Nightmares

Under The Moonlight

by

Joe Chianakas

Four Phoenixes Publishing

United States   Canada   United Kingdom

Joe Chianakas

Printed in the United States of America

First Printing, 2016

Presented by Four Phoenixes Publishing: United States, Canada, United Kingdom

www.joechianakas.com

Contents

Cover Illustration by Camron Johnson

www.camronjohnson.com

AUTHOR'S NOTE:

Camron's art is mind-blowing. We're using his work for *Rabbit in Red Volume Two*, too. His haunting blue moon piece certainly inspired some of the tales in this collection. He has a variety of talented, twisted, cool, incredible pieces on his website. If you're looking for art illustrations for any kind of work, be sure to check him out. He's a talented and professional individual, who I hope to work with for all of my publications. – Joe Chianakas

Introduction

Think about how many horror books you've read. Now think about how many horror movies you've seen. Is there a difference?

Chances are, you've seen something like ten thousand more horror films. Maybe I'm exaggerating. Maybe not. Maybe the same is true even for me.

I've learned something from that when it comes to writing. One reviewer called my first novel, *Rabbit in Red*, "like reading a movie." She visualized every scene and was lost in the story. That's exactly what I wanted.

When I write, I think of a cool idea or an interesting character. If people read my stories and say, "that would make for an awesome movie," then I've done what I wanted to do.

I dream of the day Hollywood calls me and says, "You're on to something in that story you wrote, 'The Destroyer.' We want to chat with you." Or even better, maybe someday they'll call and say, "We need some fresh ideas."

Because I feel like I have a thousand.

Every writer may tell you something different when it comes to our process, but for me, it's all about a great idea, one that you could summarize in a sentence. Think of your favorite tales. A baby survives an attack from the world's most powerful wizard. A ring gives you the power of invisibility—but at great cost. A boxer from the inner city is gifted the chance at a world championship fight. Lots of great ideas, right? All in one simple sentence. From there, it's a little more complicated. But that's how it starts.

And so begins this collection of stories. I won't preview them for you here. I want you to read them. Afterwards, can you sum up the plot in one sentence? Do you think it would make for a great horror film? Did you enjoy it?

If the answer is yes, I'll hope you'll recommend this collection to others and post a nice review online. Thank you for giving it a chance.

I'm beginning and ending the collection with *Rabbit in Red* tales. I hope you'll enjoy those stories even if you haven't read that book. The first—"Whispers and Flames"—takes place in between the first two books of the series. The last thing I'll leave you with is the first chapter of the second book (*Burn the Rabbit*, out now) and the third and final book (due out fall of 2017).

In between those stories, I'll introduce you to new worlds and characters, and hopefully plenty of new terrors.

May the horror be with you.

Enjoy.

- Joe Chianakas, May 12, 2016

"For readers, one of life's most electrifying discoveries is that they are readers—not just capable of doing it . . . but in love with it. Hopelessly. Head over heels. The first book that does that is never forgotten, and each page seems to bring a fresh revelation, one that burns and exalts: Yes! That's how it is! Yes! I saw that, too! . . . That's what I FEEL!"

—Stephen King, Finders Keepers

Whispers and Flames

A Rabbit in Red Short Story

Tara Stein's eyes popped open at the noise. Pure darkness engulfed her bedroom, but her eyes adjusted quickly. She looked out her bedroom door, which was halfway open, to the hallway outside. Jaime's bedroom was on the opposite end of the hall, and there was one bathroom in between the rooms. Tara wanted to call out to her sister, but embarrassment held her back. Instead, she peered into the dark hallway.

"It was only a nightmare," she whispered to herself. But she sat up in bed and stared into the dark hallway nonetheless. The bathroom door must have been cracked open as a thin blade of light poked into the hall. She focused on the area surrounding that one blade of light, probably just the moonlight shining through the bathroom window. A minute passed, and she exhaled deeply, thinking what a silly fool she was.

Then she saw a shadow grow. It was in the walls. Something was there, something she couldn't see or describe except for a darkness that grew bigger. She thrust her hand over her mouth to stifle a cry. Tara wanted to call out to her sister.

Jaime would know what to do. Jaime lived in books and movies about nightmares, but this was no book or movie. Tara was staring at some kind of movable, growing darkness, and she was afraid it was not an innocuous figment of her imagination. It was real, and her fear was palpable. It was as if the room had gotten colder, but she was too afraid to move and pull the blankets tighter. The thing in the dark might see her, and if it saw her, then it could hurt her.

A crashing sound echoed from downstairs. Tara, already covering her mouth with one hand, thrust the other hand upon her face too, but that didn't stifle the scream this time. A cry escaped from between her lips, and she fell back down in bed. She rolled to the side and felt the tears stinging against her eyelids. Someone must have broken into their house! What could she do? Her heart felt like it was beating through her neck and her ears, and then the light turned on in her bedroom. She let out another cry, closing her eyes tight, convinced that this was it. The home intruder had come to get her.

"Tara, what's wrong?" It was Jaime, her older sister. Jaime got in bed with her and wrapped an arm around her. "What is it? A nightmare?"

"No." Tara shook her head, wiped her wet eyes, and rolled to face Jaime. "Someone is in the house."

"What?" Jaime sat straight up and looked around. Tara was not one to exaggerate or suffer from insecurities. "What did you see?"

Tara's arm extended and pointed at the hallway. "Out there. I swear. It was . . . I don't know what but something was there. And then I heard a crashing downstairs."

Jaime stood up and looked around Tara's bedroom. She picked up a tennis racket, looked at it curiously, and then set it back down. Tara had a small vanity mirror, and Jaime walked over to that. She glanced in the mirror, her shoulder-length, leafy-brown hair disheveled from only a few hours of sleep. Tara followed Jaime's gaze. Normally, Tara would smile at the resemblance. She kept her hair shorter than that of her big sister, but it was all too obvious that they were related.

Jaime picked up a pair of scissors and nearly smiled.

"What are you going to do?" Tara asked, her mouth open wide with surprise.

"I'm gonna check the house. You wait here," Jaime stated with confidence. Tara noticed that Jaime had been a different person since Halloween, but this had not surprised her. Jaime had participated in a wild horror adventure at Rabbit in Red, a major motion picture studio in Hollywood that was run by the eccentric billionaire producer Jay Bell. Jaime and her best friend Bill spent all of fall preparing by watching horror films and reading every scary novel they could get their hands on. Tara watched a few movies with her sister, and even browsed a couple of the books. She didn't understand why people liked being scared. She loved spending time with Jaime though, but whenever Tara thought something scary was about to happen in a movie, she just played a round of Trivia Crack.

Her sister understood the addiction to trivia. After all, Jaime had spent an entire weekend riddle-solving, and then she was invited to a hands-on competition, a fright fest of horror, at Rabbit in Red. Tara remembered that when Jaime left for Rabbit in Red that she was bursting with excitement, even more so than when they saw the midnight premier of *Mockingjay*. Now that was a movie Tara enjoyed. But when Jaime returned, Tara thought that her sister had changed. Her eyes were darker, and she didn't have the same child-like enthusiasm. Something had changed in her sister, and then to Tara's surprise, she learned that Jaime would be returning to Rabbit in Red again the following year. It was something Tara didn't understand, and something Jaime had yet to explain.

These thoughts flew through her head quickly as she saw Jaime pick up the scissors and walk into the hall. Tara hesitantly crawled out of bed and followed her sister, even though she had said to wait in the bedroom. Jaime glanced back and sighed. "Just be quiet, then."

Tara walked like Jaime's shadow, closely glued to every move. Jaime held the scissors in the same way Michael Myers had held his butcher knife, and Tara shivered at the thought. But she followed her sister as they checked every room. Tara held her breath when Jaime put her hand on the doorknob to a closet or new room. What would they do if someone was actually in the house? Would Jaime really stab an intruder? Tara felt her goosebumps rise on her skin at the thoughts. Certainly, Jaime had developed a thicker-skin since her experience at Rabbit in Red, but Tara couldn't imagine her sister stabbing someone.

They heard a noise from a closet in the hallway down below. Tara thought of that awful *Halloween* movie that Jaime wanted to watch every October. In the movie, the main character hid in a closet. In an ironic reversal, was the intruder in their house hiding in the closet below?

Jaime looked over her shoulder and nodded to make sure Tara was ready. Tara shrugged. She was far from ready, but what choice did they have now? Whoever was in the house must certainly know that they were aware. If they tried to call the police, wouldn't the intruder run from the closet and attack them? If they tried to ignore it and go back to bed, they wouldn't be able to sleep. Their mother's bedroom was on the main floor, and Tara wanted to call out to her, but that meant they'd have to walk by that closet door first. A dozen thoughts went through Tara's mind, but she sighed and half-nodded at her sister. They had to move forward, right? Jaime nodded back as if reading Tara's mind and walked down the stairs. Tara held her breath.

They stood outside the closet door from below where they had heard the noise. Jaime lifted the scissors high above her head, and Tara wrapped her arms around Jaime's waist. Wasting no more time, Jaime pulled the door open quickly. Tara couldn't help herself. She screamed as the door flew open.

But the closet was empty.

"What about mom?" Tara asked.

"If your scream didn't wake her, then I hate to bother her," Jaime said, and they shared a mutual understanding as to why. It was winter, very close to Christmas. Their mother's favorite pastime was watching sappy romances on Lifetime, and now that Christmas was approaching, the dramatic television channel hosted holiday-themed specials twenty four-seven. Last night, their mother had enjoyed not one but two full bottles of wine all to herself and sobbed into a box of tissues. Christmas was a particularly difficult time for their mother. Their father had left her many years ago.

"She'd have woken up if someone was here, right? I didn't imagine it. I swear." Tara pouted.

Jaime nodded, and Tara wondered if two bottles of wine could have knocked their mother out and made her oblivious to any sound. "Let's check every room." Jaime forced a smile and ruffled Tara's hair. She wrapped an arm around her little sister's shoulders, and they explored the rest of their home.

"Thank you," Tara said when they had searched every room, "for checking."

"Of course. Do you think you can go back to sleep?"

"I'll try. But I swear I didn't imagine it, Jaime. What I saw and heard was real."

Jaime nodded in a way that made Tara feel that she wasn't crazy. "I know, and I believe you. The brain can . . . can make us see things that aren't there. It doesn't mean you didn't see it. Do you understand?"

Tara bit her lip and shrugged again. They walked back into her bedroom, and Jaime sat down on the bed with her after putting the scissors back on the vanity desk.

"Want me to stay?" Tara shook her head no but she meant yes. She didn't want Jaime to think she was such a little girl, though. Even though Tara didn't get into horror like Jaime, she also hoped her big sister would invite her to Rabbit in Red someday. "Door open or closed?"

"Open, please," Tara answered as she pulled the blankets close. She watched Jaime walk away, but she didn't think she'd be able to sleep. She grabbed her phone that had been charging on a table next to her bed. She scrolled through Instagram and yawned, bored at the same kind of pictures over and over again.

'Hey. You awake?' She decided to send a text instead. She wanted to tell Bill about her night and how brave Jaime was.

'No I'm sleep textin,' Bill replied. Bill was Jaime's best friend, but he lived far away. The two had met online a couple of years ago, and they both took on the Rabbit in Red challenge. From what Tara could tell, she thought Jaime liked Bill more than a friend, but they had never officially declared themselves boyfriend and girlfriend.

'So J about killed a dude tonight.'

'What?!'

'Yep. Grabbed scissors. Was gonna go all Michael Myers. #YouhaveacrazyGF!'

'She's your sister. And not my #GF :(What happened? Say true.'

'I heard a noise. Thought I saw someone in the house. She grabbed the scissors and went after them.'

'Are u ok?' Bill texted back.

Tara paused before replying. She had forgotten about Bill's dark past. Jaime had told her all about it. Bill had always been so funny and kind with her that it was easy to forget that he had his own demons. He really had seen a home intruder before, and more than that, the home intruder had murdered his father.

'Yeah, it was just my stupid imagination, I guess. No one here.'

'It's not stupid. When you have a vivid imagination, you become a little more sensitive to your surroundings.'

'That how u feel?'

'I don't necessarily think I have the best imagination, lol,' Bill texted back. 'But I am very aware of my surroundings, yeah.'

Tara looked around her room, and the hall, which was completely dark again except for the little light through the bathroom window from the moonlight. She remembered what Jaime said about moonlight. *The sun may be brighter*, Jaime had said. *But the moonlight—the moonlight shines upon evil. It's like spotlight to make us aware of the real life nightmares under the moonlight.* Jaime was always writing some kind of creepy story, or reading or watching a creepy story. Tara wasn't sure if those were Jaime's words or if they came from something else.

'Is the moon bright where you are?' Tara texted Bill.

'The brightest. I think that's why I'm still awake lol. It's kinda creepy.'

Tara texted Bill for a few more minutes, and then got back out of bed. She walked to her bedroom door and looked down the hall and down the stairs. Nothing to see. Nothing to hear. She walked back inside her room, pulled the curtain to her window a bit to the side, and looked out at the night sky. She missed sunshine. Winter was a terrible time of year. Even on the few days the sun was bright and the sky was cloudless, there was little warmth. She wanted to feel the sun's warmth.

Everything was less scary on warm, summer days. On a long winter's night, it seemed anything was possible. It was dark and cold for far too long.

She curled back in bed, finally satisfied that what she saw and heard was nothing like a Rabbit in Red production but rather a simple projection from her own imagination.

But just as she closed her eyes, she heard a whisper.

Her eyes popped open, but she remained still in bed, stiff as a corpse.

What had she heard? Was it real this time or was her mind playing with her again?

But she heard it again. It was a man's voice.

"Burn the rabbit." The whisper sounded like that of a snake from a *Harry Potter* story. "Burn the rabbit," it called again.

When Tara felt a cold chill enter the room, she sat up. She ran out of bed and turned on the light. There was nothing to see. She peered down the hall and the stairs again. Nothing. She ran back to her bedroom window.

From outside, the bushes on the side of the house moved. She saw a shadow ever so briefly reflected under the moonlight.

And then it was gone.

*****

Rose Dawn had never seen snow. She drove with her family from New Orleans to North Eastern Tennessee to spend Christmas with Grandma Harper. She borrowed an oversized, fluffy winter coat from Grandma and sat out in the front yard making a snow angel. She felt bright in the snow, her skin actually a few shades darker than the white as clouds fluff under her body. About a dozen family members had gathered inside, and Rose could hear them laughing. She smiled, not so much at the laughter but at the peace of being alone, even if only for a moment.

"Wake up, genius," a voice called from the front door. It was her cousin, Charles, who had recently become a Stephen King fan after hearing of Rose's Rabbit in Red adventure.

Rose sat up slowly and faced Charles. He, too, had fiery red hair with freckles to match. He was a few years younger, just a boy beginning his high school journey. Rose cherished the thought of only one more semester of high school. Soon she'd be back at Rabbit in Red. She never told Charles or her family everything that had happened. She left out the part about being kidnapped by witches and seeing her friends encounter physical harm. Her parents wouldn't understand why she'd want to return to such a place. Maybe Charles would, she thought. He still has a child's imagination. The protective and critical nature of adulthood had yet to run the imagination out of town. That's something she learned last Halloween, something that separates a youthful mind from a cynical one. She almost laughed out loud, picturing her father holding a stake like in a vampire movie and chasing a demon known as Imagination. Her father wasn't like that, really. He wasn't some crazed Westboro cult-like preacher, but when one's children could get hurt, parents can turn themselves into anything, even monsters.

So Rose kept quiet, even to Charles, about the real events at Rabbit in Red, and she counted down the days until she could see Wes and her other friends again. The truth for Rose was quite simple. At Rabbit in Red, she could become anyone, and a little danger only served to enhance the imagination. She thought JB would most certainly agree.

"So you started the second book?" Rose asked Charles.

"After the last line of book one, I had to! I've got to hide them from my mom. If she knew I was reading some book about a psycho that gets off on his mother, she'd kick my ass." Charles, wearing only a sweater and jeans, sat down next to Rose in the snow.

"I do love that last line. Wes suggested I read it. King's still got it."

"He says he has a headache. And he's asking for his mother." Charles shuddered as he quoted the line again. "I about shit my pants!"

Rose laughed, but the look on Charles' face was genuine. This was one of the many things she continued to love about horror and Rabbit in Red: getting others excited about the stories that excited her. She wished that Wes were here. He loved talking about King, and she missed him. They had talked every single night since they left California and returned home. It was nice to see his face on Skype or FaceTime, but it wasn't the same. They had only spent one weekend together—but what a weekend—and it had brought them closer together in a couple of days then many couples were after months of dating.

"What's that noise?" Charles asked, pulling Rose from her thoughts.

"Hmm?" She sat up straighter and looked over her shoulder. She could still hear the families chatting and laughing from inside, but nothing else.

"At the side of the house. Over there." Charles pointed to the right side of the house. Grandma Harper's home was the last house on the left on a small cul-de-sac. Rose stood up and walked over.

"What are you doing?" Charles asked in surprise. "What if it's a wild animal? Or . . . or worse?"

Rose smiled. Charles had definitely been reading too many King stories. But that was a good thing. Perhaps the things in his imagination are trying to scare him, but at least his imagination is working. Besides, Charles hadn't experienced what Rose had. She could handle the things that go bump in the night.

She smelled gasoline. It was sharp and pungent, completely out of place in the middle of snow. Then she heard a match strike and smelled sulfur. From the corner of her eye, the match flew forward, nothing greater than a spinning splinter with a glowing flame like an arrow head. But it was enough. It hit the snow, and the gasoline she smelled ripped ablaze. Rose held her breath. For a moment, she thought she should run or dive for cover, but she was frozen in place. The size of the fire surprised her. She had a vision of the entire house bursting into flames, but the fire was nothing really. The gasoline poured on the snow created only a few lines, and the total size of the outline was no bigger than a Volkswagen

Beetle. The shape of the fire kind of looked like a Beetle, too, until Rose saw what it was meant to be.

The shape on the snow in front of her was that of a rabbit.

And the rabbit was on fire.

*****

Notes to self—

This is kind of like a diary entry, I guess. I just need to write to think, sometimes. I wonder if people even keep journals anymore. Isn't the internet one giant diary?

I'm working on a plan, you see. I need to figure it out. I need to learn everything about them. I almost got caught by Tara and Jaime, but I slipped away. I needed to be close. I needed to see the inside of their home.

I needed to smell her.

Jaime smells like lavender. She didn't even open her eyes when I looked at her. Her sister of all people almost caught me. I still have much learn, I suppose, about all of them.

No more home visits. Not until it's time to actually . . . well, perhaps I shouldn't write that down. I've been watching them all. Online, that is. Why do people post about their travels publicly? Stupid. But stupid Rose posted about visiting family, so I paid her a visit. I almost let her see me.

I want someone to know I'm after them. They think they're brave. They think they've conquered their fears.

They don't know what real fear is. But I'm going to show them.

I stepped into the shadows of the moonlight as Rose watched the burning rabbit. I even wore boots too big for my feet and slid instead of stepped in the snow, in case anyone would come looking. But they won't. The best part was seeing Rose stomp out the fire. She won't tell her family about it either. Stupid girl. They're all so stupid. She wants to come back. They all do. And that will be their fatal flaw. So they will say or not say whatever it takes to return. They'll pretend nothing is wrong, that everything is only a game.

Right up until the moment before they die.

The man stood up and admired his hand-written notes in the yellow legal pad. It seemed so professional, and he smiled at his own thoughts. Some of his ideas may be silly. Some would get him locked up in an insane asylum or prison for the rest of his life. He didn't care. He spent every single moment thinking of ways to destroy Rabbit in Red.

And to destroy each of those kids.

He slid his fingers over the note gently, as if it were the body of a beautiful woman. He smiled, thinking someday he'll touch Jaime just like that, right before he kills her.

He couldn't wait to burn the rabbit.

AUTHOR'S NOTE

"Whispers and Flames" takes place after *Rabbit in Red* book one but before book two. Book two, *Burn the Rabbit*, is available now. The third and final book in the trilogy is scheduled to be out during fall 2017.

Learn more about the series on my website at www.frightfest4d.com and be sure to follow my Facebook author page for the latest updates: www.facebook.com/chianakas.

The Destroyer

Addie and I sat in my car late one warm winter night, two of last people on Earth who still wanted to enjoy the dirty taste of a cigarette. We were not-so-secret smokers. We tried to keep the house smelling clean, but in my 1999 piece of shit Chevy Cavalier, we didn't give a damn. Let the thing smell like an ashtray. It looked like one.

Normally, we'd have the heater on and the windows just cracked, but it was warm, especially warm for Missouri, considering it was the first of February.

"Climate change, they say," Addie told me as she took a long drag, the cherry tip of the cigarette burning bright. "Do you believe that?" She looked at me, her eyes weary from a long day of work. We'd finish these smokes then go to bed and start another same-o same-o work day in the morning. Addie was a middle school teacher. She was in her mid-twenties and had been teaching for a few years now, but she never smoked at work or in front of the kids.

I nodded. "At least we're not running the car tonight. Wasting gas and all." I took a long drag and coughed hard exactly at the same time I saw the truck down the road.

"Look at that." Addie pointed at the truck.

"What's that on the front of it?" I asked. As it approached, I could see that it was a huge semi, and it had some kind of funny face across the front grill. It was an emoji, the hysterical one, the laugh with tears rolling down its cheeks.

"Wonder what he finds so funny," Addie whispered.

I shook my head but didn't speak out loud. We were parked at the end of a cul-de-sak. We'd been renting a home here for a couple years now, and neither of us had ever seen the likes of a truck like that on our small town street. It nearly consumed both sides of the road.

"Maybe you should park in the drive way," Addie suggested.

I nodded but didn't move. The truck approached, and I felt frozen. There were only a few more houses behind me, and I wondered where the truck was going. We must have been the third house from the end of the block.

The truck crept closer.

And closer.

It approached the front of my shitty Chevy. The hysterical emoji looked so out of place, and for a second, realistic or not, I thought the truck my eat us. Like, literally, the mouth of the emoji would just open up wide and swallow the car with me and Addie in it.

"Jim, this is scaring me. Let's get inside the house."

I held up my right hand and said, "One minute. I want to see what he's doing."

The truck really did consume the road, but it didn't eat my car. It's right side rolled onto the sidewalk on the street across from us a bit, and it slid by us with maybe just a foot in between my car and the truck. I squinted and pressed my face against my window to try and see the driver's face. Just as the driver passed, a sliver of moonlight reflected over the driver's side window. But the truck's window was tinted, and I didn't see a face. That's when Addie opened her door.

"No!" I snapped. I don't know why I snapped at her, but something inside me said that it wasn't safe to go outside. "Wait."

The truck was no longer just on the sidewalk. It rolled up onto the front yard of the house across the street from ours. And then it stopped.

"Jim, I think we should call the police."

I reached into my pocket for my cell phone. As I brought it up in front of me, the truck's engine roared a barbaric yelp. I dropped my phone, and it slid right underneath the seat.

"Fuck." I sighed and reached for it. My hand his some metal bar. They make it so easy for shit to slide underneath your seat, but impossible for anyone to retrieve it, I thought. "Addie, I can't get it. Can you try?"

She bent over, her head in between my legs and reached under my seat. In any other situation, I would have made a dirty joke, but tonight was far from the ordinary.

"Oh my God," I mumbled.

"Ouch!" Addie cried as she jerked up and hit her head on the steering wheel. "What is it?"

"Look!" I pointed at the truck. Its engine shouted again.

The truck lunged forward at an impossible speed. Nothing that big can have that kind of acceleration, right? I don't even know why I was thinking of that question. Shock can do strange things to the mind.

Having parked and roared its engine a couple of times in the front yard of our neighbor's home, the truck sped through the next neighbor's front yard to the last house on the right. But when it approached that house, it didn't stay in the front yard. It turned and drove right through the house.

Not just into it. *Through it*. The house, a ranch style single-family home, collapsed completely as if a tornado had just hit. It took nothing but a second.

Was the family home? Sure they were. It's late. They were probably getting ready for bed, and then BOOM!

Gone, in an instant.

I shook my head. How is this happening? And what the fuck am I am going to do?

"Addie, the phone, now." I reached out my hand to her, but I couldn't turn my eyes away from the destruction I had just witnessed.

"I couldn't get it," she said.

"Then give me yours."

"It's inside the house."

I looked at her then, then I looked at our house, and then back at the semi. It was backing up now, slowly.

Once again, I found myself frozen as I watched the truck back up onto the street. I considered my options. I could run in our house. *Jesus, our puppy, our two cats!* Could I just leave them there? What if the truck attacked our house?

Then I looked at the keys I had in the ignition. The car wasn't running, but I had turned the radio on so we could listen to some music while we smoked. I considered just getting the hell out of there.

The semi's engine growled again, a vicious and sickening noise. Then it charged forward once again. Before I could even blink, the truck had smashed into another house, the second one from the right at the end of the street. This house blew up, boards, debris, glass going everywhere.

"Jim, what the fuck are you doing?" Addie shook me. "We have to get the hell out of here!"

I started the car and we did exactly that.

I raced to the end of the street, and I was breathing hard, as if I had been sprinting instead of driving. Then behind me, I saw that damn emoji approach. It was faster than me, and in seconds, the damn laughing and crying face was inches behind.

It's going to eat us, I thought again.

"Oh, Jim, what are we gonna do?" I saw Addie's hands shoot up and cover her face. Then I heard the cries. Her cries had always been kind of awkward. She had cries that sounded like cute sneezes. There was always a girl you went to school with or worked with who sounded like a little bird whistling when she sneezed. That's how Addie sounded when she cried.

Despite everything, despite a monster truck that had crushed and destroyed two houses and was now chasing us, despite Addie, my girlfriend, the woman I had told myself I would eventually marry, despite it all, I smiled.

Then the truck hit my shitty Chevy from behind.

The seatbelt pulled tight against my chest, and Addie moaned.

"You okay?" I transformed into the soccer mom with my right arm fully extended across her body.

She turned her head slowly toward me, the way I'd picture a lizard turning its head just before eating its prey.

"No, I'm not fucking *okay*, Jim!" She pivoted in her seat and looked behind us. The beast of a truck had slowed. "What the fuck is he doing?"

I looked in the rear view mirror and saw what Addie had seen. The truck was turning around.

"It could have destroyed us, if it wanted. I don't know what it wants, but maybe—"

I froze. I don't know how I knew what I knew, but somehow I sensed an absolutely forbidding premonition. "It's going to our house. He's gonna destroy our house. And he wants us to see." I slammed on the breaks, thrust the car into reverse, and accelerated towards the demon.

"What are you gonna do?" Addie looked pale, a ghost under the moonlight.

"I have to stop him. Oh, Jesus, Addie, our babies."

Addie screeched and another awkward cry leaked out of her mouth. "Oh, Jim, you have to save them!" To others, they may have only been one little puppy and two cats, but to us, they were our fur-babies, and I had to get to them. I can't believe I even left them, I thought. But I didn't have any choice, did I?

The truck was much faster than my shitty Chevy, but I caught up to it before it destroyed anything else. It seemed to be waiting for me. It had once again turned itself around, and it faced me as I approached. The hysterically laughing emoji on the front of its grill mocked me. Parked at the end of the cul-de-sak, with two houses at the end already destroyed, the truck simply laughed at me.

Where are the neighbors? Where are the police? Somebody should be doing something!

Addie reached over to me. "What are you gonna do?"

I turned and faced her. "Okay. I'm gonna run in the house and scoop of the kids. You hop in the driver's seat. If he comes at you, drive away. Just swerve, and you can avoid him. If he comes at the house, honk. Don't let up, just honk, and I'll know." My heart was racing, and I felt myself breathing hard even though I had only been sitting. Addie reached for a cigarette and lit up.

"I don't know, Jim. We shouldn't . . . why is this happening?"

"Why does anything happen, Addie?" She puffed on her Marlboro, and I exited the car.

I swear the emoji was animated or something. The grin looked wider. Such a sinister grin.

The first couple of steps I took were slow, and I kept my eye contact on the destroyer. Then I sprinted. I felt like I was back in school, running on the playground from the person selected as "It" as if my life depended on it. This time, though, it did.

I got into the house, and then I let myself look back. Nothing. The truck stood still. Snapping my head to Addie, I saw the glowing cherry of her cigarette.

"Chunk, Mikey, Mouth, where are you? C'mon guys!" Mikey ran to me right away. A tiny Dachshund, I was greeted by kisses and scooped him up. "Chunk, Mouth, where are you?" Cats were much more fickle creatures, and I worried they'd be harder to find. Time to bring out their kryptonite. I went into the kitchen and grabbed a pack of a hot dogs from the fridge. I opened the bag and waved it around the house. "Chunk? Mouth? Come here!" It worked almost instantly. One grey cat—Mouth—and my large orange cat who lived up to his name—Chunk—rubbed on my legs. Good, okay, now what? Shit, how am I gonna get all three out there?

That's when I heard the horn. My car's horn matched the power of the shitty Chevy. It sounded more like a dying siren, but nonetheless I knew it was time to get the fuck out. That semi had destroyed two houses in the blink of an eye. I looked behind and then I saw what I could use—a box! It wasn't very big. I had used it to carry in some wood for the fireplace, but it would suffice. I tossed the hot dogs into the box. Chunk jumped right in, but Mouth—always the more cautious of the two—looked up at me as if questioning my actions. "C'mon, Mouth." I moved Mikey to my left arm, grabbed Mouth with my right, and put him in the box. Then—and they were going to hate this but they'd have to make due—I put Mikey in with them. The cats hissed, but I grabbed the box before they could jump out. I picked it up, ran to the back door, and not one second too late either. As I stepped out back, the house exploded.

My home. Poof! Like that, it was gone.

I felt a pain in chest and a gag in my throat. I swallowed back some vomit and ran.

Every fiber in every piece of wood blew up. I ran around the left side of the house. I could barely see—it was like a huge smoke bomb, a storm cloud of debris. Addie had turned around, and when she saw me, I could see her cry. She reached across the front and threw the passenger door open. I tossed in the box of our fur-babies, probably the only babies we'd ever have. Then I hopped in the back seat. Addie floored it, and I looked behind me.

The truck had backed up after destroying our home.

It faced us.

It flashed its lights. Somehow this made the truck look as if it was winking at me.

The emoji grinned and cried in laughter. The truck backed up slowly, and before we were out of its sight, I saw the driver roll down the window.

Could it be? No, it couldn't be him.

The driver looked like my father. But my father had died many years ago.

The driver winked at me, just like the headlights on the semi. Then he rolled up the window. The last thing I saw as we turned off our street was the beast of a truck accelerate toward another house.

I turned around and shook with a feeling of absolute coldness.

Addie looked at me in the rear view mirror. "Are you okay?"

Without looking at her, I said, "No. Most definitely not."

She nodded, understanding and not understanding all at the same time.

"Where should we go?"

Out of town? To hell? Anywhere but here? I thought of lots of things, but the answer that came out my mouth surprised me. "To my . . ." *Am I really suggesting this?* I pictured the man who stepped out of the semi. "We have to go to my father's grave."

"What?" Her eyes narrowed in the mirror. "Why?"

"Just go."

"But why?" She looked at me as if my suggestion was the most shocking thing of the night. Then she continued. "I thought . . . didn't you tell me that your father tried to kill you once? That he was a bad man?"

I nodded. "Yes."

She shook her head. "First, we gotta go to the police."

"No. The graveyard. I'm serious, Addie."

I had never seen that expression on her face before. It was fear and confusion—but not at a demon truck destroying homes. It was fear and confusion directed at me.

"Just go."

"To the graveyard." She sighed. Mikey jumped on her lap and licked her face.

I shivered again. Addie didn't know it, but I knew something. Just like I knew the truck would return to destroy our house, I knew this story wasn't over. Not yet. In fact, I knew the real story would start at my father's grave.

Stories often begin with someone else's ending, don't they? I smiled and thought of that night, that night from many years ago.

I had no logical thoughts, really. Addie was probably right. We should have called the police. We should have tried to warn the neighbors. That truck—it was backing up and destroying homes one at a time.

And why?

I laughed. If that really was my father, it makes sense. When he was alive, he didn't just want to destroy my life. He wanted to destroy everyone's life around me, too.

So we raced to the grave. I needed to see it.

I needed to see that very hole where I had buried my father the day after I had murdered him.

AUTHOR'S NOTE

"The Destroyer" came to me in a nightmare.

I think the idea of a demonic semi destroying houses in the middle of the night is a cool idea.

Don't you?

We'll learn more about Jim's father in another story. I'm saving that for another time, perhaps for another collection. I hope you enjoyed not only the tale, but also the mystery behind it.

Easy Listening

"Ouch," Nicole said and pulled out the earbuds. She had been listening to Taylor Swift's Red album, and ironically enough, the blue earbuds had turned red, too. Or at least the right one did. She looked at it closely and rolled it around her hand. It had a drop of blood on the end of it, the part that had been in her ear. She reached through her purse and took out a small mirror. Trying to hold it up to her ear, she couldn't get a view of the inside. Carefully, she rubbed her index finger around her ear. Nothing hurt this time, and when she looked at her finger, there was no sign of blood.

"Huh," she mumbled. She wiped off the earbud and put it back in. She had taken these off of Bruce's desk at work. Bruce had asked her out just the other day. She had smiled and said maybe, that she'd think about it at least. Nicole liked to listen to music at work, and her cheap headset felt scratchy. So when Bruce was away in a meeting, she took his blue ones. She'd give them back. Maybe when they went out. *If* they went out.

She straightened her legs and stretched, touching the concrete below her feet and letting the thought of Bruce and his blue earbuds slip away. Coming up easily, she leaned back and arched her back. The sun was bright, but the air was chilly. Winter held onto the air like a prison guard trying to hold back spring. It shouldn't be this cold in April, Nicole thought. Not in South Carolina, for sure.

It had been a long winter, nasty. They had ice storms, snow, and temperatures she had only thought existed on TV shows like *Fargo*. Not in South Carolina. Nicole wasn't going to let the weather keep her locked up inside her apartment. She needed to run.

She had never been a runner. In college, she joked that it's only the skinny people that get kidnapped. "No one's gonna be pickin' me up and tossin' me in the back of van," she'd say and laugh.

What had happened since then? She let out at long, slow breath as she stretched her legs some more. Mama had died, that's what had happened since college. Mama who loved the buffet almost as much as she loved the bottle. That Old Country Buffet in town knew mama by her first name. So did the owners of every liquor store. Mama died of a heart attack at fifty-four years old. Fifty-fuckin-four. Nichole wiped away a tear from her eye. It had been two years since mama's death, but damn if the memory didn't always hurt like a bitch.

Nicole had been in a dressing room trying on new jeans a few months after mama had passed when she decided it was time for a change. Her usual size was a sixteen at the JC Penny, but a couple months of stress eating turned her into an eighteen. Nicole had cursed, tossed aside the jeans, and bought her first pair of workout clothes ever.

A year later, she was proudly down to a size twelve. And she ran even more because of it. Running felt good. It cleared her mind. She even talked to mama.

On this cold, April day in South Carolina, Nicole ran, rubbed her sore ear, and started her conversation with mama.

"Bruce asked me out the other day, Mama," Nicole said. She didn't care who saw her. She had her earbuds in, and she talked softly. Anyone watching her would probably think she was just singing along to whatever it was she listened to.

"I haven't been with a man since . . . well, you know . . . since Bobby." She frowned for a second, and her pace slowed. Bobby left her about a month after her mother passed. "Bobby was weak," she said out loud. "Didn't like to see me sad, I s'pose. But don't you think a strong man should be able to handle sadness?" Nicole nodded and picked up her pace. She was already close to the Neilson farm. She always ran fast by the Neilson farm. Old man Neilson's smile got a bit too big whenever Nicole ran by. It gave her the creeps.

"And now I've got stretch marks, Mama. What do I do about that?"

Nicole wished her mother could answer. She may not have made the best choices in her life, but she always had a kind heart and a sharp eye. *Quit that worryin', baby. Just turn off the lights when ya get in bed if you don't want him to see your stretchy legs.*

Nicole laughed. "Thanks, Mama."

She pictured Bruce and wondered if she should let him take her out. Bruce was cute. He had a big belly but nice arms. And who was she to judge? She had had a big belly most of her life. Maybe she'd give Bruce a chance.

Then her ears stung again. "Oww!" Nicole cried. It was the right ear again. She took out the earbud, and another drop of blood had formed. "What the hell?" She came to a complete stop and examined the earbud more closely. It didn't look like it had any sharp edges. Carefully, she circled the inside of her ear with her index finger. Checking it, there was no blood. No anything. Nicole shrugged and let the right earbud dangle. She'd have to tell Bruce he sure had some shitty earbuds. *If* she let him know she took them, that is. But at this moment, she was about to throw them away.

Leaving just one in, she turned up the volume on the Taylor Swift album and started running again.

"What's that all about, Mama?" Nicole looked up to the sky. It was gray and dark, like it had been almost every day. Nicole needed sunshine and warm weather, not this gray, cold shit.

She had made her way to a long, private rural road she enjoyed running. It was flat with just the smallest of hills near the end. Nicole liked giving it her all on the small hill, and then she'd turn around. All in all, this route was about six miles, and she could finish it usually under an hour.

Her thoughts drifted back to Bruce. It had been a long time since anyone had touched her. Maybe it was time to get over whatever issues she was having and just let him do whatever he wanted with her. She might even like it. It would certainly be better than getting her rocks off to some Fifty Shades of Shit. Laughing, she approached the hill. She took a great deep breath and charged full speed ahead. About half way up the hill, her left ear started to hurt. There was an intense pressure. It took her instantly back to the day she had had her wisdom teeth taken out. It was a pulling and a pushing inside her head, but the pressure was more intense than anything she had ever experienced.

Then she fell. Stumbling on the country road, she rolled, gashed her knee hard, and twisted her ankle. When she came to a stop, she pulled out the left earbud. It was dripping with blood. Not a drop or two like she had seen on the other, but oozing, pouring blood like a thin but powerful faucet stream. She looked down at her bruised knee and felt dizzy. Losing focus, she brought her right hand up to her left ear. Bringing her hand back, she examined the palm. Her hand was as red as an apple. Blood was everywhere.

"Mama, what's happening?"

Then Nicole blacked out.

*****

She awoke and gasped at the old man staring back at her. He was missing one of his front teeth. She'd recognize that creepy smile anywhere. It was old man Neilson.

"Sweetie, it looks like you had an accident. I saw ya up the road, just sprawled out waiting to get run over or sumthin."

It all came back to her. The bloody earbuds. The Taylor Swift songs. Telling Mama about Bruce. What had happened?

"There's something wrong with my earbuds," she managed to say. "My ear is sore." She pressed her hand against it. No blood this time, but it was sensitive to the touch.

Old man Neilson looked at her as if she were speaking a foreign language.

"Don't know nutin' about ear puds, but I called Dr. Moon at the clinic. He said he'd stop by after they closed. Didn't want you movin', sweetie. It shouldn't be long now." Old man Neilson left the room. She was in a guest room, evidently. Or one of the kids' rooms, now long grown up and gone. It was a stiff, twin bed, and she sat up to get a better look at her surroundings.

She wasn't a fan of Dr. Moon, either. Moon was pretty much everyone's doctor in this town. He had also been Mama's doctor.

There wasn't much to see in the old bedroom. She got out of bed slowly—she wasn't going to stay put in this creepy place, that's for sure, no matter who said what. But just as her feet touched the floor, old man Neilson was back with his creepy, toothless smile holding a mug.

"Sweetie, you get yourself back in that bed. I made you a hot cup of tea. This will help you 'lax sum while we wait on the good, ole doctor, awright?"

She exhaled through her nose, but nodded. She did feel a little dizzy after all, trying to stand.

She sipped on the tea, and in moments, she fell back asleep.

*****

Darkness engulfed the room when she woke up. "Whaa?" She tried to mumble, but her face felt numb. *Why is it dark? Where am I?* Her thoughts were foggy. Through the bedroom window, a sliver of moonlight appeared. *Moonlight!* Did Dr. Moon ever come? Am I dreaming? What happened?

She swung one leg out of bed, but had never felt so tired in her life. Ever so slowly, she managed to sit up. She got the other foot out from under the bed sheets and placed it on the floor. Then she tried to stand. The room felt wobbly, like she had too many cocktails. She stumbled forward and placed her hand on an old dresser for support. She hit the dresser hard, and a photo that had been on it—one of the now old Neilson kids?—fell to the floor. The frame that it was in made quite a noise, and Nicole gasped.

It was pitch black other than the sliver of moonlight. She tried to find a light switch on the wall. Moving from the dresser to the wall, she dragged her hand slowly forward. Then she felt human flesh.

Her hand was on a body, and looking up, she saw the creepy, toothless smile of old man Neilson.

She wanted to scream.

"Sweetie, you okay?"

She shook her head. *No.* No, I'm not okay. And it's not okay that I'm here. But she couldn't speak. *What's wrong with me?*

"Oh, sweetie, Dr. Moon gave you some medicine and said you should sleep, doncha remember? I said you could stay here till you felt better. The doctor didn't think you shoo be walkin' home. You'll feel better in the morn."

She stared at him. Was he telling the truth? She had no recollection of Dr. Moon's visit or taking any medicine. Her head sure felt heavy, though. And she couldn't even talk.

Old man Neilson walked her back to bed, and she swore that his hand was way too low on her back. For a moment, it drifted over her rear. She looked over her shoulder. He smiled that disturbing, toothless smile, his pale face nearly glowing in the dark.

"Back to bed, sweetie. Back to bed."

She didn't want to go back to bed. She wanted to run out this house screaming. But the moment she got back in bed, she fell asleep. *Must have been some strong medicine Dr. Moon gave me,* she thought as her eyes closed.

*****

She woke again just a couple of hours later. It was still dark, perhaps even darker, as the moonlight had mostly vanished.

I don't remember a doctor here, Nicole thought. No, something was funny. Something was wrong, very wrong. She felt more conscious now. Much more so than before. She swung her feet around and placed them both on the floor.

Then she heard a creak. In the corner of the room, there was a rocking chair. It was moving. *Had that been here before?* She didn't remember seeing it. Her eyes had adjusted well to the dark, and she could make it out: a simple, wooden, old rocking chair. The same chair she had seen old man Neilson sitting on a hundred times as she ran past the farm while he sat on the front porch.

He was sitting it once again.

His face was sharply white, like a ghost.

He smiled.

Nicole screamed and stood up.

Old man Neilson grabbed her, looked her in the eye, and for a moment, she froze.

And then he screamed, too. Loud and shrill, he yelled right in her face, and she cowered back as if she had just been smacked in the face.

"In bed, sweetie, in bed," said the old man when he had finished screaming.

He tossed her with great force back into the bed. He was significantly stronger than his skinny body looked. It was as if decades of working on a farm gave him permanent strength. He pinned her down easily. She tried to struggle. Maybe it was the medicine—*there was no medicine, fool*—but she still didn't feel like herself. *It was the tea!* She thought of it just then. The old man must have put something in the tea.

She tried to calm her mind, to think smart about the situation. What could she do to get out of this?

She laid still and he spooned her from behind, one arm over her body, his hand brushing up against her breast. Her heart and mind raced. *Mama, what do I do?*

She thought of Bruce in the office and the blue earbuds she took from his desk.

"It will help me relax if I can listen to my music," she told him. "You can listen to it, too. With me, if you want. I just need my earbuds."

He breathed down her back and neck, and it gave her chills. Several deep breaths. Then he finally answered. "What are these ear things?"

"They play music. Like headphones. They sync with . . . my . . . with my music." She sighed. She almost said phone. *Have to be careful, Nicole!* "We just lay and listen to the music. That's all." *What does he want with me? I'm too weak to fight, at least right now. I need to buy some time.*

"Where they at?"

Nicole bit her lip. "I don't know. I had them in my ears when I . . . when I fell. Did you take them?"

She heard a grunt. "Oh. Yeah. They looked like hearing aids. I got 'em." The old man left the room, and Nicole sat up. Too fast, Nicole, too fast. She was dizzy again. The old man returned quickly, holding the blue earbuds.

"How these work?" Old man Neilson sat down on the bed.

"Put one inside your ear, like a hearing aid, I guess," she said and handed him the one that was in her left ear. The one that had caused all the pain and all the blood before she passed out.

Now she needed her phone. "You have my phone?"

His head snapped toward her and he glared.

"Not to call anyone," she tried to assure him. "You play the music from it."

He reached into the back of the pajama pants he wore. Gross, Nicole thought. He pulled out the phone from his rear.

"You can't call anyone, sweetie, not tonight."

"I'll show you how to use it. I promise."

He looked at her incredulously, but he turned on the phone.

"What do you like to listen to?" Nicole asked.

"Sumthin' easy on the ears," he said.

"All right. Push the button that says 'music.' See that?" It took three tries but he pushed it.

"Now press play." It was still on her Taylor Swift album. That would have to be easy enough.

The music started to play. She let the right earbud dangle close to her ear, but she didn't put it inside.

She let old man Neilson cup her breast as he pressed himself against her. She tasted vomit her mouth and swallowed hard. Closing her eyes, she counted her breaths, one at a time. It wouldn't take long, right? Something had to happen.

Just like something had happened to her.

"Starlight" played, a song from near the end of the album. Nicole heard the old man scream as Swift sang, "He said look at you, worrying so much about things you can't change."

She turned around and pressed her hand hard against his ear, making sure the earbud didn't come out.

Old man Neilson screamed louder, and, even though it was dark, Nicole could see the blood pouring out of his ear. She pressed her hand even harder. The old man's eyes grew bigger and bigger, until they were nothing but white, and then he passed out. His body was limp against hers, and she couldn't have been more grateful.

The thought had popped in her mind earlier: she should have known better than to take something off of Bruce's desk at work. She decided she would go out with him, to at least figure out what the hell was wrong with these earbuds. Nicole worked as a legal assistant in the office, but Bruce—Bruce's position was always a secret. He had an awful lot of meetings behind closed doors with people who looked like government officials. She'd have to find out what exactly Bruce did.

But for now, Nicole started at old man Neilson. She put a hand over his chest. His heart was still beating.

She put both earbuds in the old man's ears, cranked her music, and held them in place with her hands. She stared at the old man, blood continued to ooze out of both ears this time, but she didn't care.

She let the album finish, and by the time it did, the bed had soaked with blood.

Then she took her phone and called Bruce.

He answered very groggily. "Hello? Nicole?"

"So, tell me about those blue earbuds that were on your desk."

AUTHOR'S NOTE

I was out walking one day, listening to my music, when I felt a sharp pain in my ear.

I smiled and thought—there's a story here.

Next time you feel a pain in your ears when your earbuds are in, I recommend taking them out and checking them for blood. You just never know.

Restless

"It's time," Eddie told his partner, tossing a half-smoked cigarette out of the cracked window of his SUV.

"How long they been out?" Donald asked as he zipped up his black hooded sweatshirt.

"No movement for thirty minutes. Keep an eye on your smart watch. You know I'll text if there's a change."

Donald slipped on a pair of leather gloves that were darker than the night that surrounded them and exited the passenger side of the SUV. They had been parked near the end of this cul-de-sac for over an hour. He looked at his smart watch, making sure it had enough battery life, and saw that it was nearly 3:30 a.m. Eddie and Donald had been watching the houses on this block, in a wealthy suburb outside of Chicago, for several nights, timing the sleep and activity patterns of its wealthy and oblivious residents.

Eddie's SUV resembled what Donald called a soccer mom vehicle, and Eddie had said that was perfect. *"You don't park an ugly van or cheap car in a rich neighborhood, especially at night. But a nice vehicle like this Enclave? Perfect," Eddie had told him.*

Donald approached the house on the left, a tight box of a mansion, windows piled on top of one another as if to say *sure, no one needs this many windows, but we want to show you our lucky riches.* "Can't wait to take the riches from you," Donald whispered out loud as he approached the front door of the McMansion.

The majority of the houses in this neighborhood were protected by a state of the art alarm system, but that didn't worry Donald. *"Never trust a door to door salesman to protect your home," Donald had told Eddie when they discussed the idea.* Donald had been playing this adventure for quite some time, and he took a job as a door to door alarm salesman and installer. He had walked this neighborhood last summer, and thanks to the never-ending plethora of violent news stories from their big city neighbor of the north, it wasn't difficult to persuade a few wealthy homeowners into taking extra precautions on security.

"It's a sad world we live in," Donald had told them. "We steal from our neighbors and kill the innocent." He would shake his head and sigh, and sometimes he'd even get a little tear to form in the corner of his eye if he was talking to a mother. "I can't stand it! But I will fight it. Mr. and Mrs. Smith, I invested in Peace of Mind Securities to protect the American family. Let me show how our security system is the most advanced in the world."

Donald sold Peace of Mind to the entire neighborhood, and of course he had the digital means of accessing the systems from the touch of a button. As he approached the house, he clicked that button on his watch, and just like that, he had disarmed the security system.

Eddie texted 'still good' from the Enclave, and Donald entered the home with the ostentatious and superfluous windows splattered across the front like stars on the flag. Although the home was filled with items any common thieve may want, Donald only wanted one thing: access to the home safe his Peace of Mind Security also had installed.

"Here," he had told them during the sales pitch, "you can stash emergency cash, all your important financial and personal documents, firearms, anything for which you'd want absolute security. And only you can access it. It unlocks with your fingerprint. No one can hack the code." Except for me, *he'd think and stretch a long used-car-salesman smile across his face.*

The beauty of his plan was that he'd be in and out, and no one would suspect a robbery until the homeowners checked the safe. By that time, be it the next day or even weeks later, Donald and Eddie would have cash, guns, jewelry, valuables, and the necessary information to hack into bank accounts and rob people of their entire life savings.

Inside the house now, Donald approached the safe he had installed on the main floor. *"You don't want a safe in your bedroom. That's where the criminals expect it,"* he had said. Once again with the ease of a button touch, he opened a door to a lifetime of valuables. He started taking the contents of the safe and put it into a briefcase when his watch blinked with an alert from his partner outside. 'Restless,' the text stated.

Donald cursed in his mind, but kept calm.

'Both restless,' a second message from Eddie warned.

Donald straightened and listened. The house was silent, the husband and wife whose kids were old enough to have kids of their own slept alone in the master bedroom, just above where Donald stood. He would wait until Eddie texted that they were asleep again. Even if they got up to pee or get a drink, Donald could hide and wait. He had made sure to close the front door. The alarm had been deactivated. Little Mr. or Mrs. Nobody would go tinkle or get a 3:00 a.m. snack to contribute to their obesity and waddle back to bed. Donald would creep out the moment Eddie alerted him that it was safe.

He stood waiting and texted Eddie '?' wanting an update.

'Still restless.'

Donald shut the safe. He'd have to return to it later, and to be safe, he crept into an empty room, Mr. Nobody's office from the look of it, and waited.

Seconds later, another message read: 'AWAKE!'

"Shit," Donald mumbled. He may have joked in his mind about the 3:00 a.m. snack, but this was the first time he'd have to actually wait for his victims to fall back asleep.

'BOTH AWAKE NOW!' another alert screamed at him.

Donald listened and heard footsteps, followed by the sound of urination, and then a flush of the toilet.

"Honey, will you get me a glass of water?" a woman's voice called from above.

"Yeah, just a sec," the man replied.

The man walked downstairs, past the hall with the safe, right beyond the office where Donald hid, to the kitchen. Donald heard the clinking of ice fall into a glass from an automatic ice maker and then the splash of water into the glass, eerily similar to the urination he heard moments ago.

The man went back upstairs. "Thank you," Donald heard the woman say.

"Uh huh," the man said.

"My knee is bothering me," the woman told him. "I need to walk it out."

"Uh huh."

"Go back to sleep. Oh, I hate this knee. It hurts when I use it and it hurts when I don't. I'll be back in a bit."

Donald heard footsteps come down the stairs again, lighter this time. 'STILL AWAKE,' Eddie texted. *No shit*, Donald thought. He examined the contents he had placed in his briefcase. He had a stack of cash and some jewelry, but not everything. He didn't have time to grab the documents from the safe, the priceless personal information that would allow him to hack into bank accounts. He breathed hard through his nose. He wanted it all, and he'd wait for the old woman to go back to sleep if he needed to.

Or maybe I'll put her to sleep. Whatever I have to do. He smiled and was also somewhat shocked by his own thoughts. *Could he hurt someone? Would he?* He thought about it a bit longer. *Well, we'll see, I guess.*

Then he heard a TV turn on in the living room, and after a moment, he poked his head out to see what the woman was doing.

He got a flash of her large ass up in the air and had to stifle the urge to laugh. She was in a down dog yoga pose. *3:30 a.m. in the damn morning and she's doing yoga to a home workout video. Jesus.*

'One asleep, one awake,' Eddie texted him. Well, at least the man fell back asleep. Now to figure out what to do with this woman.

He watched her move from down dog to up dog, the only two poses whose names he actually knew, to a series of other silly stances. After several minutes of this, Donald's patience slipped away like the night before him, and he crept out of the back office. He crawled to a stop behind a couch in the living room where the woman was now balancing on one leg, her arms driving diagonally up to the ceiling.

If she turned around right now, she'd see his face. A sliver of moonlight shot through the window, illuminating Donald's smile.

Now's my chance. Let's see what I can do.

He jolted out from behind the couch, grabbed the mat she was standing on, and yanked it off the floor.

"Ohh!" the woman cried and stumbled forward, her head smacking the entertainment center that housed the TV. She hit the corner hard and fell to the floor. Donald straightened the mat, ran back to the safe, and emptied the rest of its contents.

'Both asleep!' Eddie texted and Donald laughed. He walked past the woman, now unconscious on the living room floor, and just to be safe checked for a pulse. Feeling a beat of life still pumping throughout her body, he laughed, picturing the husband finding her like this and thinking of what the old Mr. Nobody would say. *"You and that yoga in the middle of the night! Sooner or later you'd take a fall like that!"* Days may pass before they discovered that their safe was empty, and if Donald was lucky, the old couple would never even connect the dots.

A splattering of blood tricked down the woman's forehead, just a little, like a coffee stain from the bottom of a mug on a table. She'd be okay. Probably. *If not, what's it to me? Get what you want, whatever it takes. Next time, it may take more than a fall to get the victim to go back to sleep.* Donald grinned at his thoughts and walked out the front door back to Eddie's Enclave.

"That was close," Eddie said. "We never had anyone wake up like that before." He closed the program on the tablet he had used to monitor their victims' sleep. It was Donald's proudest piece of technology in the Peace of Mind Security, but this part of course was not something he told the buyers. When he installed the systems, he hacked into their Wi-Fi and Bluetooth technology, and he always paid close attention to which homeowners wore a smart watch, a Fitbit, or any kind of activity and sleep tracker. Those were the only homes they robbed. All they had to do was park close enough to hack into the Wi-Fi and the Bluetooth technology of the devices, and they could monitor their sleeping patterns to know when the innocent homeowners were awake, restless, or sleeping. They could even access sleep history to determine how long they slept on average and what times they generally woke up in the middle of the night. It was the perfect piece of technology to invade homes.

"Where to next?" Eddie asked.

"Let's see who else is sleeping tonight," he said. "That last house . . . the restless old farts . . . it all felt so . . . so exciting." Donald's eyes widened, he licked his lips, and he smiled. Yes, he wanted more. Even the restless ones. He could handle that, too.

Eddie drove, and Donald checked his notes from previous observations.

"That one looks good," Donald said pointing at the last house on the left. He accessed their sleep and activity tracker. *Been asleep for four hours. No restless moments since midnight. Alarm set for 7:00 a.m. I think they're due for a restless moment.* Donald's smile showed nearly all of his teeth as he thought about what he was going to do next. He was hungry, but not for food.

"Isn't technology wonderful?" Eddie asked. Donald nodded and laughed as he exited the vehicle.

He had never been more awake in his life.

AUTHOR'S NOTE

It's a simple idea that could produce a thousand stories. We love what technology and all of our smart devices tell us.

But what could they also tell others?

Sleep well. The only reason to be nervous tonight is if you wake up restless. So whatever you do, don't do that.

Joe Chianakas

A Halloween Poem

I saw a spider on the door

As I reached for the knob.

It spun its web, trapped my hand,

And turned it into one pink blob.

I ran to the back door,

Only to be greeted by an army of wasps.

They flapped by my shoulder,

Reminding me that nature is boss.

I stared at an empty box

Left in my living room.

And then it opened on its own.

The flaps– like a ghostly flower– bloomed.

Spiders, wasps, and ghosts in boxes,

All of this is true.

To cleanse myself from evil.

I jumped in the shower with you.

Then my lover said, "come to bed."
So I crept into the sheets.
But a clown's face greeted me
With teeth as bloody as beets.

I screamed when it bit me,
And the spider cast a web.
Then the wasp formed a nest
And the clown in my bed said:

"Happy, happy Halloween
I hope you like my friends!
We'll be here with you
Until the very end!"

A smiling jack-o-lantern
Sat on the window sill.
And with blood running from my face,
I knew that I was so very ill.

It was Halloween, all right,
Our greatest fears had come to be.
I had spiders, wasps, and clowns
Horror was all I could see.

But I laughed as blood soaked the sheets

And told them they were fools.

You're messing with the wrong man.

I break all of Halloween's rules.

And so I became the horror

That walked down the street,

To torment and freak

All of those who were meek.

On this night, our fears came true.

Do you have strength to fight them?

Because on one night, you will see

The evil only you can imagine.

Knock Knock Knock

Knock. Knock. Knock.

I tried to sleep but no sleep would come.

There was a tapping, a rapping, a ravenous pounding.

And I couldn't take it anymore.

I threw the covers off of my bed.

Then put my bare feet on the floor.

The floor was cold.

Not middle of the night cold.

But cold as death.

I jumped back in bed,

And pulled the covers up just below my eyes.

Knock. Knock. Knock.

"Who is it?" I asked.

A foolish question.

I knew it was death.

Too cold to be anyone else.

I pulled the covers over my head.

But then the room began to glow.

It was a nightmare under the moonlight.

White light, then blue light, then red light.

No, it was an orange light, an apocalyptic light.

I pulled the blanket tighter.

But the tighter I pulled it,

The brighter the room got.

And the hotter.

I couldn't breathe.

I was . . . choking, dying. I couldn't fight it.

I threw the blankets off.

And . . . it was dark again. And cold again.

It was fire. It was ice.

Knock. Knock. Knock.

"Go to hell!" I shouted.

And then I laughed.

This is hell.

Death has already won.

So who the fuck is knocking on my door?

I stood up. The floor cold. The room dark. My head hot.

I walked to the bedroom door.

I swung it open and snarled.

But no one was there.

Knock. Knock. Knock.

It wasn't coming from my bedroom door.

It was coming from my closet.

My face got hot again.

Sweat dropped onto the cold floor.

My heart beat in my throat.

I swung the closet door open.

There she was.

My love.

The one who made my face hot and feet cold.

She was all gagged and tied up, barely breathing.

She stomped on the floor.

Knock. Knock. Knock.

I picked up a baseball bat that I kept close to my bed.

I hit her in the stomach.

Knock.

I hit her on the back.

Knock.

I hit her in the head.

Knock.

I smiled.

Drool fell from my lips onto my love like one last kiss.

Maybe now I could sleep.

I got back into bed.

Closed my eyes.

Sleep took me away.

Until . . . until . . . once again . . .

Knock. Knock. Knock.

PC Load Blood

The nightmare woke me up. Flashing lights, red and blue, and a bright reflection, like sunshine on a mirror, pierced my eyes. My head hurt, and the heartburn returned, too. My stomach was like a washing machine's high speed rinse cycle whenever I had this dream.

I sat up in bed and stretched. "The fucking washing machine!" I threw in my work clothes a few hours before bed but had forgotten to put them in the dryer. "God dammit."

My bedroom was on the third floor, top of the house. The washing machine was in the basement. I glanced at an old alarm clock I kept around. Don't know why. Everything I needed was on the cell phones nowadays, but I liked the soft red glow of the numbers in the middle of the night. "Ugh." Two in the fucking morning. All right, all right, all right. Better wake up and put the damn clothes in the dryer. Better than not having clothes to wear.

I laughed. I wonder what my co-workers would think if I just showed up naked one morning.

"Oh, Ernie finally went bonkers!" I laughed at my own high pitched voice. That's what Vanessa would say. She liked the word bonkers. Everything was always bonkers. The boss, the customers, the computer. If it was a little odd, it was bonkers. Of course, I suppose me showing up in my birthday suit would be bonkers.

I swung my legs out of bed and put my feet on the floor. The carpet was soft. I put a hand in my whitie tighties and adjusted myself. I wondered if Vanessa liked her men in whitie tighties. My ankles cracked and my knees popped as I walked out of the bedroom. I don't know why I was thinking of Vanessa at all. She was a Millennial, at least I think that's what they call them. I'm somewhere between a Baby Boomer and a Gen X'er. I think. I don't know, but I do know I can still get my motor running, whitie tighties or not. I could give Vanessa a real ride.

I laughed again. Must have eaten something odd. The nightmare came back, and I can't stop thinking about some fresh-out-of-college whore.

You don't know if she's a whore, a voice said to me.

"Aren't they all?" I answered out loud.

I walked down the first flight of stairs and paused in the kitchen. I've got Tums somewhere here. Some Tums and a shot of whiskey, that ought to help the gut. Or at least help me sleep.

I opened up the cabinet where I kept a few meds, mostly just aspirin and Tums. Shaking a couple out of the bottle, I threw them in my mouth and then went to liquor cabinet.

It was empty, though. "You stupid sonuvabitch." They made me give up drinking years ago. The doctors, I think. Or was it someone else? Must be losing my mind. I shut the door to where I used to stash the liquor. Too bad. That would have helped me sleep.

I thrust my tongue over the top of my bottom teeth, trying to get out the pieces of the Tums that gut stuck. Smoothie flavor, I think they called this one. "More like shitty flavor." I chuckled again and opened the basement door.

Nothing like a pitch black basement to welcome you after a nightmare in the middle of the night. I inhaled hard through my nose and flipped the light switch. A soft, buzzing light brought to life the creepy first floor. Water damage from years ago left a constant mildew smell. The paneling had been torn off, and there was nothing but a layer of concrete separating me from the dirt of the earth. I walked to the washer and dryer. I grabbed the clothes from the washer—my fancy uniform that I wore over at Baker Industries. Far from any kind of bakery, Baker Industries was all about pharmaceuticals. I think, anyway. I don't know. I wore this uniform and fixed things like leaking toilets and mopped the floors and looked at Vanessa's ass whenever she got off it from her comfortable desk to do actual work.

She had a nice ass. Tight but big, the kind you could just sink your teeth in to.

I tossed my uniform into the dryer.

That's when I heard the noise.

Something from the back of the room. It was an electronic beep, piercingly loud. It made the lights flicker.

"Someone there?" I asked. I swallowed hard. Not sure what I'd do if someone actually answered back.

Another beep. It was coming from the corner.

I slid my feet over the dirty, concrete floor. Shuffling slowly, I never let my feet off the floor.

Beep. Beep. And then it breathed. Or it sounded like a breath.

Beep. Beep. Breeeaaatheee. Beep. Beep. Breeeaaatheee.

I saw it. The white nearly glowed in the dim basement. "What the fuck?" I kicked at it. It was an old printer. Some small HP printer I had for an old desktop computer Lord knows how many years ago.

Out of its mouth, a piece of paper came. It looked like a white tongue sliding out of grey lips.

I picked up the piece of paper.

`Hello Ernie.`

"What the hell is this?" A sharp pain pierced right in the middle of my forehead. I rubbed it with my left hand and crushed the piece of paper with my right.

A second sheet of paper stuttered through the printer's mouth.

310. Now.

I sniffed hard and tasted blood. I rubbed under my nose and sure enough, there dripped a few drops of blood. The headache intensified.

A third piece of paper shifted and rumbled ever so slowly towards me. I grabbed it, but didn't read it. Looking more closely at the printer, I saw its old cord. It looked like it had been chewed on, which was weird. I never had a dog. But what was weirder: the cord wasn't plugged in to anything. The printer was operating without electricity somehow.

That made my head hurt even more. Then I looked at third piece of paper.

*****

"Morning, Vanessa." I smiled, teeth wide as a kid who just found his first dirty magazine. I didn't think yoga pants were part of the dress code here, but she wore them tight and snug. Snug as a bug in rug.

"Ernie." She said it the way you talk about the weather on a rainy day. Like "cloudy" with an eye roll and a sigh. "The boss left a note for you." She picked up an envelope and held it out with her right hand without ever making contact with me.

I wanted to say the thoughts that were bouncing in my head, but we did just have that sexual harassment seminar last month. Can't even be cute and call her "sugar" anymore. That one got me a one on one with Human Resources.

"Thank you, Vanessa." *I got a plunger that can unclog whatever's shoved up your ass.* I took the envelope and walked to the break room. My head felt fuzzy, like I had been drinking all night, except I hadn't.

What had I done last night?

I remembered the dream, the flashing lights in my head. I remembered having to get my old ass out of bed and putting my uniform in the dryer. And then . . . and then? Must have went back to bed and got a few hours of sleep, I guess.

No, wait. I remember the moon. It looked . . . blue. Is a blue moon a real thing? But it wasn't just the moon. The moon had a face in it. A face that laughed at me. A face that told me to hurry the fuck up before I get caught.

Get caught doing what?

I opened up the envelope.

`Clean up, 310. Do it again.`

I poured some hot coffee into a foam cup, hot and black, no sugar needed. Then I got my throne on wheels, which consisted of a cheap garbage can, mop and bucket, and enough cleaning supplies to disinfect a small country. Strolling to the elevator, I looked at the note again.

That font. That type. It looks just like . . .

Ding.

The elevator doors opened. I pushed my throne on wheels into the elevator and pressed the number three.

Ding.

The doors opened again, this time to a number of cubicles. People dressed in suits rushed from one end of the floor to the other. I had no idea why they were always in such a hurry. They always ended right back in the same spot as they started. I pushed my throne on wheels to the back of the floor to office number 310.

I coughed when I opened the door. "Jesus, that's a lot of disinfectant." I put a hand over my mouth and gagged. Did I clean this room yesterday? The note said to do it again. I clean so many rooms, it's hard to keep track, but I don't know why I'd use so much disinfectant.

That's when I saw the blood on the floor. There was a puddle in the back of the room, near a metal desk. I looked behind me quickly, worried that someone would come in.

Why would you be worried?

I shook my head and rubbed my temples. "Shut up," I said and took out the mop. No, maybe I better use some paper towels first. Wipe it up then mop it up, that's the best way to deal with blood.

How the fuck do you know that, Ernie?

My head hurt again, and this time I rubbed my forehead. Then I got down on my knees and wiped the blood clean off the floor.

"What the fuck?" There it was again, under the metal desk.

Again?

It was an old HP printer. I used to have one of those. It took nearly a minute to print out just one piece of paper. The paper stuttered out, like the main kid did in the Stephen King movie about the clown. The kid stuttered and shook to get a word out. The old printer did the same for paper.

"Wonder why it's under this desk," I mumbled to no one.

"Hey, Ernie, the boss told me to—"

"Fuck!" I hit my head hard on the side of the desk when I heard Vanessa's voice.

"Bonkers! What happened in here?" Vanessa asked.

I looked at the paper towels I had been using to wipe up the blood. They were soaked in red.

"Dunno," I choked out. "Just doin' what I was told."

"It looks like blood." I smiled when she leaned over to get a closer look. Her tits could knock a fella out.

"Maybe it's Kool-Aid," I suggested and licked my lips. They felt awfully dry.

"The boss sent me here to—what's that?"

Beep. Beep. Breeeaaatheee.

"Why is there a printer under the desk?"

I shrugged my shoulders and rubbed my head. The pain was getting worse.

Beep. Beep. Breeeaaatheee.

The printer ejected a piece of paper. Vanessa gasped.

"Ernie, what's this about?" She pursed her lips and looked at me like I just tried to feel her up or something. She handed me the paper.

Hello Ernie. Hello Vanessa.

She stood there as the printer went back to work. Nearly a minute later, a second sheet of paper came out. My head hurt even more. I started seeing flashing lights. Red and blue. It was harder to focus.

Blood, Ernie. We need her blood.

I smiled at her. Incredulous, she stood there, as if literally frozen.

"I don't under—"

I stopped her before she could continue. The pain consumed my head, and my knees popped as I jumped off the floor. I put my right hand behind her head and my left on her ass. I pulled her tight and squeezed her tighter. I hugged her as hard as I could. She struggled, and the more she struggled, the better I felt. I sniffed her hair and her neck. She smelled fresh, and I needed to taste her. I needed to taste her now.

I bit into the side of her neck like she was nothing but a piece of meat.

She would have screamed, but her face was pinned to my chest. There was no air for her to take in.

I let the blood pour on everything but me. I'd get a few splashes here and there, sure. It seemed like I was up every night doing laundry. Couldn't avoid it with a job like this one.

When there was nothing left, I put her body flat on the floor. I laid down next to her, by her side, and put an arm around her.

I smelled her hair. It still smelled fresh.

I ran my fingers through it and wondered what she was going to say. What was it the boss wanted?

Then I laughed.

I knew very well what the boss had wanted.

Anytime I got distracted—like with the booze or, in this case, with a hot broad—he took it away.

Every fucking time. I should have known better than to talk about Vanessa and get called into Human Resources.

The boss wanted me all to himself. He made sure nothing clouded my mind whenever he needed to send me a little message to clean up his messes.

There was always a mess to clean up. There was always someone's blood he needed.

Always.

Black Widow

Jeff ran. He ran faster than he ever had in his life. He felt like he was flying, his feet barely touching the concrete. Adrenaline has that effect.

Something was behind him. He had a feeling that he was being watched when he first started walking through the cemetery. It was a beautiful evening. The sun was setting, turning the sky into a kaleidoscope of orange and purple hazes. Jeff had something on his mind, and his favorite way to tackle a nagging idea was to get out of the house and walk. Just keep walking until everything makes sense.

But his walk turned into a run when he thought someone was watching him. *Maybe I'm just being paranoid?* He looked around and didn't see anything. He slowed to a jog, and let his thoughts drift.

She had asked him out. Melanie, a beautiful and fun high school junior, texted him: 'Ok, so here goes. I like you. You know that. I think you like me too. But one of us has to say it. So, go out with me? Make this official?'

He stared at the text message. There was no smile on his face. He couldn't reply, not yet. He didn't know how to say what he needed to say. He wanted to say yes, but he had a dilemma. It was that dilemma that brought him to the cemetery to run and clear his mind.

They had met several months ago at a high school dance. He smiled at the memory.

Both had gone with a group of friends, but neither had a date. Jeff wasn't much of a dancer, but his favorite song came on. "Baby Got Back" by Sir Mix a Lot. Jeff's friends pushed him on the dance floor. They had seen him jump and dance and sing to this song for years in the privacy of their own homes. Jeff was extroverted only to those he trusted and hung out with privately. In public, he preferred to be a fly on a wall.

Melanie had giggled when Jeff's friends pushed and pulled him on the dance floor. "C'mon!" they shouted. "Do your dance! Don't be lame!"

Jeff had smiled awkwardly and his face turned red. He felt him arms and legs shake with nervousness, and butterflies were hosting their own dance party in his stomach. Jeff had one dance: he kicked his legs side to side in a fury of speed. It was the speed that awed Jeff's friends, and the look on his face that made them laugh. Jeff took a deep breath, and then he did it. He did it for his friends, and he did it for himself. He wanted to be the guy who didn't care what others thought, the guy who could have fun without worrying what others would say. He stuck out his tongue like Michael Jordan, and kicked his legs side to side.

"Yeah!" his buddies had yelled, and they jumped in and tried that side to side dance, but they were slow. It was like a bunch of sprinklers surrounding a waterfall.

Melanie had laughed and walked closer. When the song was over, she grabbed Jeff's shoulder. "You're crazy!" she told him. "And I love it." Jeff smiled shyly back and managed a small "thank you." Melanie stuck by his side the rest of the dance.

"Hey," she said. "I'm having a few people over later. We're gonna watch a movie. Wanna come?"

Jeff's friends, overhearing her invitation, nudged him forward. "Yeah, sure," he replied. And that was the beginning of their friendship.

For weeks, they sat together at lunch and hung out on the weekends. Never alone though. Jeff was either with her friends, or Melanie was with his. Until last night that is.

He ran harder in the cemetery. This was how we processed things. He let the memory of last night wash over him.

They had watched a movie just the two of them. They sat next to each other on Melanie's parent's couch. She snuggled close to him and put her head on his shoulders. He felt his heart beat fast again, like he did when his friends forced him to dance. He liked that feeling, but he was afraid. During the few moments he was brave enough to sneak a glance at her, Jeff caught her staring back and smiling. He smiled, too, and she moved even closer toward him, resting her hand on his knee. She rubbed his leg gently, and Jeff froze with nervousness and excitement. She glided her hand up his leg, high near his hip, and let her hand rest dangerously close to something else. He felt himself get excited, and when he snuck another look at Melanie, she was smiling even wider. There was a bright light from the moon that night, and it rested on Melanie's face as she smiled at him. He leaned in and kissed her. She kissed back hard. Then she spread open her fingers, and her pinky grazed right over his stiffening penis. He swallowed hard and his heart beat harder. She just left it there and kissed him. All they did that night was kiss, but her touch—he wanted more of that. He went home that night a happy young man.

He slowed his pace to a walk in the cemetery and re-read her text. He wanted to make this official, but they didn't have much time left this school year. Jeff was a senior, but she was a junior.

Melanie, it seemed, would be his first real girlfriend. The one that maybe he'd lose his virginity to. Jeff just wanted to run and think and make sure whatever he did, he did right.

He liked Melanie. That wasn't the problem. The problem was that this could be his first serious girlfriend. And unfortunately he was also planning on moving in a few months. After graduation, he wanted to escape the Midwest more than anything in his entire life. He wanted to live near an ocean, and he had applied to any school that was near the coast. Should he say yes to Melanie and enjoy a few months? What was the worst that could happen?

He thought of these questions and what—if anything—he should tell Melanie. And then he felt that burning sensation on the back of his neck again. The feeling that he wasn't alone. His skin formed goose bumps and he swore he felt eyes burning into the back of his head.

He stopped and looked around. There was a rattle in the grass beyond him, a whisper in the woods, branches cracking under heavier weight. He paused and stared off beyond the road, where larger woods embraced the cemetery. Another branch cracked. The wind seemed to stand still, and Jeff's mind sharpened to a perfect focus. He counted his breaths and focused on the area where he heard the branches break. Ten slow and controlled breaths later, nothing happened. Convinced it was a squirrel or his imagination, Jeff moved on.

Out of nowhere, he heard footsteps trying to sneak up behind him. Before he could turn around, someone pushed him hard. Jeff tripped over his own feet and yelped. He landed hard on the ground, but bounced right up. Turning around to see who had pushed him, Jeff saw a masked figure. It wore the ghost face mask from *Scream*, and it revealed a long, sharp butcher knife in its right hand.

And so Jeff ran. The adrenaline he felt on the dance floor and the adrenaline he felt when Melanie first snuggled up to him was nothing compared to this. His feet glided across the round and turned sharply into a trail in the woods that would exit close to his neighborhood. The one advantage he had was that he knew these trails and roads like the palm of his hand.

But he tripped over a long, metal grave hook in one of the paths. He screamed as his face hit a fallen tree branch, bloodying his mouth and nose. He pushed off the ground with his hands, taking a brief moment on his knees to look at his surroundings.

The masked figure was already there. "I knew you'd come this way. I thought the grave hook should do the trick," it laughed. Confused, Jeff looked at the large grave hook, something perhaps that was stuck in the ground near a tombstone to hang flowers. Looking closer, he saw that one end of the hook had been forced in a log so that the entire hook was a few inches off the ground, high enough to trip someone but not too high as to be easily noticed.

The figure took off its mask.

"What the hell?" Jeff cried.

"I was sitting in my car outside of your house," Melanie said, throwing the mask on the ground. "When you said yes to my text, I was going to surprise you and come running in. Maybe do things to you that you've never done before. But you didn't reply." Her face twitched as she talked. Jeff felt a shiver down his spine. "You left the house. Toward this damn cemetery you're always telling me about. I knew what that meant. It meant you had to think, and if you really wanted to be with me, you wouldn't have to *think* about it. You just would have said yes."

She stepped toward him, slowly raising the knife above her head.

"What the fuck? Melanie—"

"You like this mask?" Her body shook now, as she interrupted him. "My brother left it in the car, along with this knife. You know how he's always playing with his Halloween masks no matter what time of year it is. And always playing with things he shouldn't, like this." She laughed and dangled the knife in front of him. "I drove to the cemetery when I saw you leave. I know the paths you take. It's not the first time I've watched you." She smiled, and Jeff saw crazy in her eyes. How had he never seen that before?

"I won't have you break my heart, Jeff. And I won't let anyone else have your heart either."

"Melanie, wait!" he cried as she raised the knife higher over her head. Jeff started to get up off his knees, but it was too late. Melanie plunged the knife into the side of his neck.

He felt the blood shoot out. It was as if the arteries in his neck had become a powerful hose. He watched the blood cover the side of his body, and he knew in this moment that there was no future. No college near an ocean. He'd never lose his virginity.

Melanie knelt down on her knees, wrapped her arms around him, and pulled him close against her chest. He felt himself weaken, and he knew he would die. "We could have had so much fun," she said. She laughed, pulled away from him, and put in her earbuds. In his last waking moment, he listened to her sing. She stood over him now and sang, "Gonna love ya, gonna love ya, like a black widow, baby."

She bent over and kissed him, and then he closed his eyes. Forever.

Burn the Rabbit: Rabbit in Red, Volume Two

The following is a special preview of Rabbit in Red Volume Two, Burn the Rabbit. *I hope this opening chapter will motivate you to continue to follow the rabbit.*

Chapter One

His forehead glistened with sweat from a feverish nightmare plagued by a single image: the rabbit soaked in blood, a constant reminder of his warped past and a harbinger of a crumbling future. Each day he looked in the mirror and the reflection that stared back at him twisted in agony. Only wicked thoughts could make him smile now, so he'd contemplate sweet revenge and grin at the possibilities.

He had a simple morning routine. Pouring a scalding cup of coffee, hot enough to burn off any normal person's taste buds, he enjoyed the bitter taste that accompanied the pain. Pain was good. It would harden him, make him tougher, make him invincible to Rabbit in Red. Carefully holding a newspaper article about JB's Rabbit in Red Fright Fest from last year, he read it over and over again. If asked, he could recite the words JB had said, the twisted, manipulative language used to paint a picture of imagination and heroics.

"Bullshit," the man said. JB wasn't imaginative and those kids weren't heroes. JB was a villain and those kids were his prodigies, little slices of his madness, clay being shaped in the image of a mastermind host. He drank more coffee, burning his mouth a little each time. He had as many blisters as he had yellow stains on his teeth. After the events of last year, he'd let himself go.

After his coffee, he moved to the living room and turned on the TV. He had saved a number of televised news stories and interviews on his DVR. He picked one each day to watch and recited the words along with the interviewee. Today he watched an interview of Jaime, and like all of the contestants, the now soon-to-be first year students at JB's so called Horror College, he studied their body language and non-verbal behavior, too. He was determined to learn everything about them.

Because he planned on destroying all of them.

"What has JB told you about this Horror College?" a reporter asked Jaime.

"You can imagine JB likes mystery," Jaime said, laughing her carefree laugh, "so he's been ambiguous. But we know we'll be leaders. We'll be creating horror, designing sets, simulations, and stories much like JB did for us last Halloween for the initial contest. We will be inviting new participants, too. We're all flying out to Rabbit in Red Studios early this summer to prepare. During the first couple of months, we've been told that we'll help design a new contest for this Halloween, and then we'll begin more formal studies in the fall. As formal as JB can get, that is."

She brushed the hair out of her eyes. Her leafy-brown hair danced just below her shoulders now. It had grown out since last fall. The man smiled and watched closely. What did her hair smell like. Innocence? Did innocence have a smell? It wouldn't smell like that for long.

"So JB will be having a contest like last year every Halloween?" the reporter asked.

"That's my understanding," Jaime said. "It will be completely different each year, but still some kind of challenge. We need fresh blood every year."

She laughed again, and so did the man watching. *If fresh blood is what you want, I'll give it to you.*

"What happens after the next contest?"

"We'll study and create. I'm hoping we'll get to make our own movie."

"Why do you want to return to Rabbit in Red? Quite a few people, and I'm one of them, consider what JB did last year to be unethical. To be, well, almost evil."

Jaime smiled. "We thought the same at first. There's always a little madness in any genius. But I'm returning, not because of the madness, but because of that genius. We'll learn things no traditional college or textbook could teach. It's all hands-on creation."

She put both hands on her hips and held eye contact with the reporter. She looked strong and confident, especially when she took a deep breath, the man thought. He enjoyed watching her chest move.

The interview continued, as they all had a tendency to do, by reviewing the most exciting and scariest parts of last year's contest. Footage previously broadcast on frightfest4d.com, JB's website, showed images of Jaime Stein in a game chamber as Ash from *Evil Dead*, cutting off her own arm in a virtual simulation, then jumping to a live action battle where she smashed a bottle over a stunt actress who played Annie from *Misery*.

But the man had seen enough of that. He watched Jaime's smile, the focus in her brown eyes, the way she blinked and took a short breath before answering questions. She was smart. Maybe the smartest of the four who had been selected as first-year leaders. That was why he studied her as much as he could.

But he'd be lying if he said there wasn't another reason. Sure, Jaime was attractive, and maybe he'd feel just a little guilt after he hurt her. Maybe he'd give her a chance to like him first. Maybe he could tell her that the way she brushed her hair out of her face aroused him. She'd be the last one he'd destroy. He pictured what could happen. He'd pin her down on the floor and wrap his arms around her neck. Then he'd offer her a chance of redemption, if only she could feel for him what he felt for her.

Thinking about her this way, he decided he would spruce himself up. In the bathroom, he took out a toothbrush and scrubbed vigorously. He wouldn't lose the blisters or stop drinking scalding hot coffee. The pain was necessary, but he could cover up the pain like makeup hides a pale face. He could be one person on the outside and someone entirely different on the inside. Wasn't that the way most people were anyway?

Jumping in the shower, he washed hair that had been unclean for days. It was a hot spring, an early summer really. The schools had recently closed, and he spent most of these past few days inside without air conditioning, bathing only in his own sweat and stink.

He continued with his normal routine, the shower a temporary distraction, and proceeded to the kitchen. Turning on two burners on the stove, he placed a pot of water on one and ran his hands over the other. The flames felt good. Like the blisters in his mouth, he wanted to deaden his skin, to stifle all feelings, to immunize himself to pain. When the water started to boil, he'd drop his hands in deep, keeping them there as long as he could. Each day, he was able to hold them in the boiling water longer and longer. He'd grimace and even scream on occasion, but it felt good, like pain from hot sex, or so he imagined.

Then he'd return to his bedroom and take out a black, leather-bound notebook. On the first page, he glued a picture that had been taken from Rabbit in Red. It featured all original nineteen contestants with JB in the middle. Jaime, Bill, Rose, and Wes were of course directly in front of JB. Clenching his fists, he simply pondered all that he would do to them and then wrote those ideas in his notebook.

JB had sent a packet home with everyone last year that included the theme, and the media had already begun discussing the possibilities as to what this year had in store for first-year students and new contestants.

"Burn the rabbit," the man whispered. "If that's what you want, JB, that's what you'll get." He grinned at himself in the mirror.

He could clean up nice when he had to, and he had more than one costume in his closet. He could become anyone he wanted to be.

Then why do you stay you?

Shut up!

His thoughts yelled back and forth at one another. He turned on the water in the shower again. He couldn't get enough hot water. Not the hot that relaxes you at the end of a long day. He needed to feel pain. He needed to feel what they were going to feel. Taking his clothes off, he looked in the mirror.

Would Jaime like this sight?

He rubbed his chest, feeling the muscles that could pin Jaime to the ground—no, that *would* pin her to the ground! His hand glided over his belly. *She'd like that pressed against her*, I'm sure. Then his hand dropped lower. *Oh, yes. This was the treasure he'd give her, and she was going to love it.*

He stepped into the scalding-hot shower again, and let the water pour over his head. He inhaled the steam, and just stood there. Minutes later, he heard a voice.

"Honey, I'm home," a female voice called from the living room. "Where are you?"

He heard the voice over the water pouring on his head in the shower, but he didn't respond. Now that she was home, he closed his eyes and imagined he was someone else.

"Honey?" The voice was closer, and soon a creak from the bathroom door alerted him that she was entering the bathroom. "Oh, you're showering. Good. How is your cold?"

"I feel better," he said.

"It's this wicked weather," she told him. "These temperature changes. Didn't we just have the heat on last week? And now we need air conditioning, but the damn thing isn't cooling. It's no wonder you've been in bed sick for so long. Well, I'm glad you feel better. And I'm glad you're showering. I didn't want to tell you, but you were beginning to smell." She giggled.

He tried to laugh back, albeit a fake laugh. Having her by his side was necessary. He was never really sick, but when the madness overpowered him, it became a convenient excuse. She'd give him space, and he could wallow in his ideas. But the summer program at Rabbit in Red would begin soon, and the first years, as JB called them, would be returning. He needed to be strong. He would eat her cooking, go out with her in public, smile, and pretend the world was normal, when on the inside all he could picture was the beautiful destruction of fire.

"Do you feel like eating?" she asked. "I picked up some groceries. I have your favorites. I'll make some if you feel like eating."

"Yes, I can eat." Trying to remember his manners—he had to get accustomed to this façade—he added, "Thank you."

"Great! I'll get started in the kitchen." But she hadn't left the bathroom. Instead she paused for a moment, and he wondered if she might peek in the shower to check on him. After all, this shower was the first time she had seen him out of bed in days. He wandered around the house when she was gone, but otherwise, he wanted to be alone. He wanted the time to think and plan.

"I love you," she said finally, and he heard her turn around, getting ready to leave.

He looked down at his naked body as he scrubbed the dirt from his skin. Although he had been getting used to it and had actually liked it—it was like a shell, like armor—he knew he needed to keep up appearances and clean himself up. He saw something else when he looked down, something he typically only felt when he imagined himself on top of Jaime, his arms wrapped around her neck. He was aroused.

"I love you, too, Mother," he called back.

When he heard the door close, he shut his eyes, leaned his head against the wall, and let the stream of water pour down his back. He pictured Jaime. Would she want him the way he wanted her?

Or would he have to . . . could he even . . .?

The thought rose slowly, but when it entered his mind, it was like thunder. *Do I have what it takes to kill her?*

He smiled. The thought excited him. Reaching down with a calloused and hardened hand, with an image of Jaime in his mind, he pleasured himself in the shower.

AUTHOR'S NOTE

The next thing I want to share is the lyrics to a punk rock song called "Enter the Rabbit."

I wrote the lyrics. Obviously, I love writing, but it was extra cool for me to write a song. The dudes who brought the lyrics to life are extra special to me. Logan Kiesewetter, James Wylie, and Kyle Hamon make up an awesome pop punk band called Terribly Happy, and I'm proud to call them friends.

You can listen to "Enter the Rabbit" for free and browse their other work, including their first full album called *Modern Life*, at http://terriblyhappy.bandcamp.com. "Enter the Rabbit" and all of Terribly Happy's music is perfect to listen to with your earbuds in during nice walks in the woods or a cemetery. (And any time of course, but if you read all of the stories in this collection, I hope you'll appreciate what I did there.)

Their music rocks. Go listen, buy it, and keep supporting cool artists.

Joe Chianakas

Enter the Rabbit

Can you face horror's greatest monsters?

Will your fears ever be conquered?

That monster in your closet makes you shiver

It's not as scary as the one in the mirror

An axe awaits to break the chains

It opens a world of twisted games

Evil saunters without and within

Not even heroes live without sin

Enter the Rabbit, the rabbit in red

It's a celebration with a splat of dread

Passion turns to panic, fun turns to fear

The rabbit cheers, the horror will never disappear!

Can you face horror's greatest monsters?

Will your fears ever be conquered?

That monster in your closet will make you shiver

But it's not as scary as the one in the mirror

Have you been haunted, haunted by the past?

A lasting image sealed in a mental cast?

Our nightmares open a dangerous portal

It's a reminder that we are all mortal

The bruises of childhood, they linger on

Far after the black and blue are gone

Locker room jokes and mean girl swagger

Stab you in the back with a metaphorical dagger

Can you face horror's greatest monsters?

Will your fears ever be conquered?

That monster in your closet makes you shiver

But it's not as scary as the one in the mirror

A buzzing of bees on a summer afternoon

Trigger a memory, a loved one gone too soon

The rope curled like a snake hides a secret

It will tear you apart into a thousand fucking pieces

There are memories that always seem to haunt

They are buried deep, buried but not forgot

Can you face horror's greatest monsters?

Will your fears ever be conquered?

That monster in your closet makes you shiver

But it's not as scary as the one in the mirror

Enter the Rabbit, the rabbit in red

It's a celebration, a celebration of dread

Passion turns to panic, fun turns to fear

And the rabbit cheers that the horror will never disappear!

AUTHOR'S NOTE

My beautiful mother passed away on September 3, 2016. *Rabbit in Red* is dedicated to her and my father, who passed away several years before.

I watched my mom suffer through lung cancer, and she never smoked a day in her life. She picked it up through second-hand smoke, no joke. I hope if you smoke that you don't smoke around those you love. Go outside, please.

It was a rough couple of months that followed, a roller coaster really. Two weeks after her passing, *Burn the Rabbit* released. I attended several signings and events and tried to smile. It wasn't easy.

What was even harder was writing. The first time I tried to write anything creative at all was the following song I want to share with you. A local band called Liverpool and the Contractions asked if I'd work with them on a song like I did with Terribly Happy and "Enter the Rabbit." I love collaborative projects, and I said yes. So I sat down to write a song that captured the theme of *Burn the Rabbit.* But this was also the first thing I wrote after my mother passed. The lyrics work well for both.

I've been told the song will be called "Rabbit" and will be on Liverpool and the Contraction's debut album, set to release spring 2017. I don't know how much of the lyrics will change between now and then, but here it, raw as can be, for you.

Down the Rabbit Hole

Burn Burn Burn Burn Burn Burn Burn Burn

Passion, and fires, and burning desires
Fire destroys and fire inspires
It's a hunger, it's a war, we always want more
Till our passions become nothing but ashes

The time will come, for all of us
We cannot hide from the reaper
Where we go, only the fools know
Will you rest in peace or burn in pieces?

Do happy endings exist?
Doesn't everything just die?
It all comes to an end.
Love and life, so fragile, so finite

Passion, and fires, and burning desires
Fire destroys and fire inspires
It's a hunger, it's a war, we always want more
Till our passions become nothing but ashes

Slide down the rabbit hole
Enter a world of darkness
The fires will show you the way out
Only if you're willing to burn

Love changes us all, changes us all
So does death, death changes us all
And what will become of our lives,
If all that we love dies?

Passion, and fires, and burning desires
Fire destroys and fire inspires
It's a hunger, it's a war, we always want more
Till our passions become nothing but ashes

Will you burn the rabbit in that rabbit hole?
Will you fight for the ones you love?
The best of us can fail, the worst can win,
Life is a fire, changing with the wind

The darkest hour is just before dawn
Even the worst fires burn out
Ashes to ashes, dust to dust
What will become of all of us?

Passion, and fires, and burning desires
Fire destroys and fire inspires

It's a hunger, it's a war, we always want more
Till our passions become nothing but ashes

Burn burn burn burn burn burn burn burn

AUTHOR'S NOTE

Finally, I will leave my *Rabbit in Red* fans with a taste of what's to come in the final book, *Bury the Rabbit*.

I'm currently editing the book. The first draft is complete, but it's got a long way to go before it hits shelves. Still, for those of you who follow along and support me, I hope giving you the first chapter of the final book is a nice reward.

MAJOR SPOILER ALERTS HERE. If you have not read Burn the Rabbit, stop what you're doing, pick up that book, and read it BEFORE you go any further.

SERIOUSLY!

Okay, still I know some of you will read on anyway. So I'm going to do my best to wipe names. Anytime you see me write, "SPOILER" in place of a name, you'll know it's because I'm trying my best to encourage you to read book two before jumping ahead and reading this preview of book three.

Now, for those who have already read *Burn the Rabbit*, enjoy!

Bury the Rabbit

Rabbit in Red Volume Three

SPOILERS AHEAD: PLEASE READ *BURN THE RABBIT, RABBIT IN RED VOLUME TWO*, BEFORE CONTINUING.

This book is scheduled to release fall of 2017.

Chapter One

During the year that followed the original Rabbit in Red contest, Dexter Lange morphed into something like one of the lesser known characters of *The Walking Dead*. No, he walked like the dead. After his adventure at Rabbit in Red, he wasn't invited back. Instead, Dexter went back home to Seattle, Washington.

He had finished high school with passing grades. He couldn't remember what class was what, but he had a way of staring at teachers that earned a pass just so they wouldn't have to deal with him ever again. That's the one plus side to school shootings, Dexter thought. Look hard enough at someone, especially in a high school, and they'll back down.

Images from the first year contest consumed his mind. Witches, clowns, and . . . even spiders. The spider had dropped on his forehead. Then it had climbed down his nose and almost danced near his eyeball. How did JB know he was afraid of spiders?

He shook his head as he paced his bedroom on a cool winter's day. He had just received a text that changed everything. He read it and re-read it. Could it be true? Could Rabbit in Red have actually been destroyed?

He sat down on the bed he grew up in. While his old "friends" returned to Rabbit in Red, Dexter spent the year at home. His parents didn't question him. He told them he would take classes online, that he didn't want to deal with people, including them. Dexter only had to open his eyes as wide as possible. His mom would choke, his dad would blink hard, and they'd leave him alone in his bedroom.

Sitting on his bed, staring at the text that just appeared on his cellphone—*it's gone. RiR. Burned to the ground*— he thought back to that Halloween weekend, the only experience he had at Rabbit in Red. He had replayed that weekend in his mind over and over again. Even as he tried to eliminate the old visions, he still pictured himself holding a knife—what had turned out to be a fake knife—and stabbing Daniel's father over and over again.

Of course, the man dressed as Daniel's father had turned out to be JB. It was all a big game, and Dexter had lost. He stared at his teachers when they asked him about late homework the same way he had stared at JB that Halloween weekend. His eyes had said, *You know I can kill, old man. The knife may have been fake, but my actions were real. Now I know, too, that I have what it takes. And one of these days, I'm gonna fuckin' kill them all.*

At the end of that first year contest, JB had gathered them all back in Rabbit in Red's commons to explain. He had a bunch of bullshit to say. Stuff about overcoming fear, becoming a team, helping one another, blah fuckin' blah.

Dexter had stared at JB then and wanted to scream. You want to overcome fear? Sometimes you have to pick up a knife and plunge it through someone's heart! Especially if that someone was going to hurt you.

JB had invited those assholes to lead his so-called horror college. Bill, Jaime, Wes, and Rose. Sycophants, that's what they were. Sickos and sycophants. Almost everyone got invited back. JB had even let Daniel return, but he had let his brown-nosers make that decision for him.

And what about Dexter? Did *I* get to return?

"As for you, Dexter, you and I will have a conversation in private." That's what JB had said to him in front of the other first year Rabbit in Red contestants. But Dexter was never invited back.

He started to think of that conversation—more like a lecture—that JB had given him. No, no time to dwell on that conversation again.

He rolled over on his bed and re-read the text message.

It's gone. RiR. Burned to the ground."

How many times have you replayed that conversation with JB, Dex?

You know how many times. Every damn day.

But did you ever do it?

Get out of my head!

Dexter let go of his cell phone, threw up both of his hands, covered his ears hard, and squeezed. The voices were getting louder.

JB had known something about everyone. He had known their pasts and their fears. Maybe he knew everything. In their private conversation, he had asked something very special of Dexter. *It would be my redemption, if I choose to do it. For the time being, I'd just watch.*

As the summer after graduation had approached, he knew the first year students were working on the new theme. JB had called it "Burn the Rabbit." Dexter laughed out loud in his bedroom, thinking of the text message on the phone. It was as if it were meant to be.

So last summer Bill, Jaime, Rose, and Wes and the rest of the ass-kissers put their teeny tiny brains together and came up with Hellfire.

Dexter had to admit it wasn't half bad.

He had watched every news story he could, and he had followed along with any updates JB had posted on frightfest4d.com. Hellfire took a traditional haunted house and turned it into something that would literally make most people shit their pants. Enhanced by the Rabbit's Eye, an ordinary haunt could turn into anything—it could make the participant feel like they were falling or even on fire. The Rabbit's Eye was virtual reality on steroids. Yes, that was the real genius of Hellfire—it had tricked their brains into making them think they were feeling pain.

Dexter's jealousy raged. How he would have loved to try it.

Dexter watched the stories about the new recruits when they had joined. There was Brandis, who had become the new love interest for Jaime. That made Dexter laugh. He didn't give a shit about love, but anything that would piss off Bill was great. There was Carol, who had a huge girl boner for JB. That part of her made Dexter sick, but she was pleasant on the eyes. Then there was Diane—Dexter respected her. She got hurt and came back with a vengeance. Dexter had laughed when he heard about Jimmy. He didn't give a shit who the boy wanted to love, but he found it rather appropriate that Jimmy appeared to have a thing for Daniel. There were several others, but Dexter's mind drifted to SPOLIER. What a surprise that turned out to be.

Dexter had seen right away that something wasn't right with SPOLIER. What's that old saying? People can't see what's right in front of their eyes?

Moving from his bed to his computer desk, Dexter browsed through photos on frightfest4d.com.

"How did they not see this?" He spoke out loud as he looked at SPOILER.

What a year *Burn the Rabbit* had been. Dexter knew JB had made every effort possible to keep the scarier stories out of the public eye. Dexter knew this because he never saw any news stories about Tara Stein, Jaime's kid sister, who had been kidnapped and nearly burned alive. He knew that a so-called horror professor had been murdered. He knew that Diane, one of the new recruits, had nearly been killed. And of course there were other deaths—Donnie Chase, the assistant who dressed as Samara, being the one that really caught his attention.

Dexter looked at their pictures online, then turned his attention back to his phone.

He had known all of this because of the texts.

He smiled and thought of JB.

"I learned a trick or two from you, master," Dexter said with a snarl. He loved that he had someone on the inside keeping him updated. Dexter may not have been a big player last year. He watched from the sidelines and waited patiently for his turn to play.

That time had finally arrived.

Fooling someone online really was too easy.

A fake name, a fake picture, and lots of compliments: he could have gotten anyone to talk.

Dexter understood that the people at Rabbit in Red weren't typically the coolest. They spent their days with noses in books or eyes on movies. Not really with a whole lot of other people.

You have beautiful hair, he commented on someone's Instagram post.

Before long, he had made a friend.

And that friend was inside Rabbit in Red and told Dexter everything he wanted to know.

He knew something was odd about SPOILER, but he didn't say that. That's their mystery to solve.

Once people started dying, it all got very interesting, very fast. Dexter would stare at his phone at night when he couldn't sleep, hoping and waiting for such a text. How great would it be if he received a text that read, *OMG, Bill's head got cut off*. Or, *U won't believe it—Jaime hung herself.*

Dexter snorted. That would have been great.

But today—on this cold winter's day in Seattle—Dexter felt happier than he had in over a year.

He replied to the text about Rabbit in Red.

What happened?

Then he waited. He hated waiting, but he had gotten so good at it.

We're outside. RiR is on fire. Literally.

Dexter texted back: *Is everyone okay?* He bit his lower lip and hoped for the worst possible answer.

I don't know.

God dammit, go find out! He inhaled deeply through his nose. First, I better play the game, he thought.

Are you okay?

Not hurt but my brain's a mess. This is crazy.

Good, the bitch is okay. I need to know more.

Can I see? Call and put me on FaceTime. Of course, Dexter would hide his face, but he'd love to see what was going on. He'd love to see Rabbit in Red turn into ashes.

K.

Dexter sighed. He hated the fuckin' *K*. Lazy.

Seconds later the phone rang. He answered, and the camera on the other ended pointed directly at the studios.

"See?"

"Jesus," Dexter replied.

Through the bitch's phone, Dexter saw the old Rabbit in Red studios—a place the size of a city block or maybe ten city blocks—crumble with flames and smoke. He had to force back a laugh. That's what JB deserved. Let his dreams burn to the ground. Let all their dreams burn to the ground!

"Rose! Rose is inside!" That was Wes's voice Dexter heard. It made his smile grow.

There was commotion and panic. His little spy did a good job keeping the camera on all of those fucking rabbiteers.

A few moments later everyone drew their attention to someone walking up to the group. She came from the outside, not the inside. And where have you been, Jaime?

Then Dexter heard Bill ask, "Blood? Jaime, what happened?"

"It's not my blood," Jaime said back. This caused more of a commotion, and Dexter tried to focus on what he could see. It looked like Jaime had blood all over her body. But it wasn't hers? That's too bad, Dexter thought. Whose was it?

"I did what I had to do. We're safe now. Finally," he heard Jaime say.

"I have to go," Dexter's friend said into the phone.

"Wait. Who else is missing?"

"Looks like Rose and JB got trapped inside. Oh God, you think they're dead?"

Dexter forced back his grin and shrugged. "Text me as soon as you know more." The his friend disconnected.

Leaning back on his computer chair, Dexter laughed out loud. He couldn't stop it. The laughs morphed into a roar. His entire body convulsed.

"We're safe now. Finally," Jaime had said.

This made Dexter laugh even more.

The dumb bitch had no idea what was about to happen. All of the events today . . . fucking icing on the cake. Rabbit in Red burned to the ground. Looks like one of their good friends and the wizard behind the curtain may be dead and out of the picture. Hell, it looks like Jaime must have gotten rid of SPOILER—and in quite an interesting manner. He sure wished he could have seen that fight.

"As for you, Dexter, you and I will have a conversation in private."

Dexter thought once again about his final conversation with JB.

Tears were now rolling down Dexter's cheeks, and they sure weren't tears of sorrow. He was laughing so hard he could barely breathe.

Oh, if only Jaime knew what JB had told Dexter back at Rabbit in Red.

"You're not safe. Not by a long shot," Dexter said out loud.

Dexter stood up and walked to his closet. He bent over, grabbed a duffel bag, and started to pack.

It was time to pay a visit to his old friends. Maybe he'd get lucky and catch a funeral or two on the way.

BURY THE RABBIT is scheduled to release fall of 2017!

113

Until we meet again (and we will meet again), thanks for reading *Nightmares Under The Moonlight.*

www.joechianakas.com

www.facebook.com/chianakas

www.ingramcontent.com/pod-product-compliance
Lightning Source LLC
Chambersburg PA
CBHW070315120726
47910CB00007B/2487